'What's happ[...] last fifteen yea[...]

Savannah watched his face change and he stepped away until there was some distance between them.

'I grew up.' He looked at her and smiled briefly. 'According to my ex-wife, I became harsh, a loner and refused to be tied down.'

Savannah added, 'You also became a very good doctor.'

'Thanks.' The comment was dry.

'Maybe you just haven't found the right woman yet. One day you'll find her, get married and have children.'

Theo laughed bitterly. 'Having children will make everything all right, will it?'

'I said, with the *right* woman.'

'What about you, Savannah? Could *you* be that woman?'

Fiona McArthur lives with her ambulance officer husband and five sons in a small country town on the north coast of Australia. Fiona also works as a midwife part-time in the local hospital, facilitates antenatal classes and enjoys the company of young mothers in a teenage pregnancy group. 'I'm passionate about my midwifery and passionate about my writing—this way I'm in the happy position of being able to combine the two.'

Now that her youngest son has started school, Fiona has more time for writing and can look forward to the challenge of creating fascinating characters in exciting medical romances for her readers to enjoy.

Recent titles by the same author:

MIDWIFE UNDER FIRE!
DELIVERING LOVE

FATHER
IN SECRET

BY
FIONA McARTHUR

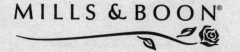

All the characters in this book have no existence outside the imagination of the author, and have no relation whatsoever to anyone bearing the same name or names. They are not even distantly inspired by any individual known or unknown to the author, and all the incidents are pure invention.

*First published in Great Britain 2001
Harlequin Mills & Boon Limited,
Eton House, 18-24 Paradise Road, Richmond, Surrey TW9 1SR*

© Fiona McArthur 2001

ISBN 0 263 82701 1

*Set in Times Roman 10½ on 12¼ pt.
03-1101-43368*

*Printed and bound in Spain
by Litografia Rosés, S.A., Barcelona*

PROLOGUE

'THE judge said he was better off with me. I'm his mother. So put the money in the account every month and you can see him when I say you can.'

The Blue Mountains shimmered in the sunlight, but the shadowy depths of the thickly wooded gullies mirrored the darkness inside him. Theo McWilliam wondered how he had ever married Marie. He'd thought she was Snow White with her long black hair, creamy skin and those red, red lips. He'd fallen hard and married her straight away. She'd been so sweet in the beginning, and so plausible to the judge at the end. But her black heart showed clearly now. The selfish witch had his son but certainly not because she loved him as a mother should. No, Marie was just using Sam to get back at Theo.

At first there had been no problem seeing his son, as long as he hadn't kept Sam overnight. Marie had agreed for Theo to take Sam for the day on most weekends because it had suited her. Then it had changed. The money hadn't been enough.

Lately, when he'd driven the five hours to Sydney to pick Sam up, he'd found the house empty. No one home even to ask.

Sometimes she'd cancel at the last minute and the more frustrated Theo became, the more it seemed to amuse her.

5

Now it had come to this.

He'd planned some time with Sam on the farm at Bendbrook for several months. Marie had reneged again, just as Theo had arrived in Sydney to collect Sam. To have this time with his son snatched away had ruined Theo's holidays—not to mention the gut-wrenching part of it—and he was scared Sam would forget who his father was.

Theo fought the urge to tuck the boy under his arm and run. They could find somewhere new to live. Let *her* try and find *them*. He could taste the adrenaline in his mouth but his lawyer had warned him against it. 'You'll lose him for good,' he'd said.

He had to do this the right way. He would wait for the time that he could take Sam home permanently and never again have to worry whether or not his son was happy in Sydney with his selfish mother. But time passed slowly in limbo, and Theo wondered how long he could postpone the rest of his life.

CHAPTER ONE

SHE was almost there.

Savannah Laine could feel her pulse quicken. In the past, she'd been the visitor here but this time the valley opened its arms to welcome her home.

The sun shone despite the unaccustomed chill for October. Stretching in front of her was an undulating vista of tree-studded, rolling hills, divided by the thick serpentine coil of the Bendbrook River as it wound its way from the mountains of its birth.

She'd always thought of it as the most beautiful valley in the world. But maybe that was because she had people who cared about her here.

The deeper into the valley she drove the narrower it became. Once past the tiny post office at Upper Bendbrook, the road became a thin, dusty ribbon that sprayed a cloud of billowing brown powder behind her as if to disguise her passing.

Finally, she arrived and she couldn't help sighing in relief. Her dust-covered Subaru bumped across the cattle grid and up the twin tracks of the driveway to the house.

Savannah swallowed the lump in her throat, stepped out of the car and filled her lungs with the tangy aroma of lemon-scented gum-trees and the sweetness of wisteria. Despite a slightly forlorn tinge of neglect, the farmhouse looked the same as it always had—welcoming.

She stood on her uncle's verandah, looking out over his paddocks. No, *her* paddocks, she corrected herself. A copper-coloured hen ran across the boards beside her and she smiled. She was a country girl now.

Benson, her mother's black miniature poodle, yelped and cringed as the monster squawked past. Savannah reached down and scooped him up one-handed and she could feel his little heart flutter against her fingers.

Now that he was safe, he yapped belligerently at the trespasser.

'Benson the Braveheart comes to the rescue. I feel so much more secure.' She watched the hen cluck down the verandah steps. She patted Benson's head.

'Before we do anything, I'll ring Mother to say we've arrived.' Not that her mother particularly cared, but Savannah would go through the motions anyway.

Benson tilted one ear at her and yapped again.

Savannah sighed. 'I know. But I promised.'

She unlocked the door and stepped into the gloom of the house. Not bothering to turn on the light or pull a blind until she'd completed the task she wasn't looking forward to, she crossed to the old black wall phone and dialed the number. Finally her mother answered the phone.

'Laine residence.'

'Hello, Mother, it's Savannah.'

'Yes?'

'Bridget mentioned you wanted me to ring when I arrived safely.'

'Did she?' Savannah could clearly visualise the vague stare as her mother tried to remember if she'd said such a thing to her housekeeper. Then she would shake her head and smile, and decide it was unimportant.

'So you're at that place.' She said it as if she could detect an unpleasant smell. 'It seems a waste to have the downstairs flat empty now. It seems like you've only just moved back in with me. Just because one man let you down, that doesn't mean you have to run away on your own and leave your mother.'

'I'm not on my own. Benson's with me.'

'Benson who?'

Savannah sighed. 'Benson the poodle. He *was* your dog, Mother. Remember?'

'Oh, yes. Lovely little black thing. I'm glad he's happy with you, dear. Anyway, there's always a home here if you decide to sell the place for whatever you can get for it. I'll mention to Bridget you've arrived safely. Thank you for ringing.' The line went dead.

Savannah felt like a telephone salesman with a product not required.

She squeezed the little dog. 'Why do I leave myself open for that?' Then she shrugged and pushed it from her mind with the ease of long practice. 'Bridget would have worried.' Benson tilted his head but didn't answer.

'Well, I'm excited.' Now Savannah turned to survey the inside of the house. She pulled the string on the nearest blind and the sun streamed in to illuminate the swirling dust motes in the air.

Alone again. Except for her brave warrior dog.

Maybe she was mad, but for the first time in a long time she did feel at peace. She didn't need to please anyone but herself. Typically, even in eternal sleep, her uncle had saved her sanity.

The next two hours passed in pursuit of dirt and drifts of spiders' webs, and for someone who hated housework, Savannah scrubbed the little house until it shone. She sang along to the same early Slim Dusty records her uncle had collected. They'd always sung when she'd been a child here and the two of them had yodelled their way through the household chores.

She'd just swept the last of the leaves off the verandah when Benson barked. She glanced up and the dust dried in her throat. A man was walking up her driveway. And she was here, alone. She looked around the verandah and finally at the broom in her hand. Not exactly a deadly weapon!

She moistened her lips and swallowed. Take a deep breath, woman. Either she was going to live here, be self-sufficient and confident, or she could high-tail it back to the rat race and lock herself in her mother's downstairs flat. She held the broom in one hand, caught Benson up against her chest with the other and drew herself up to her full five feet nothing. Then she waved. Even aliens could come in peace.

He didn't wave back. Great. She bit her lip.

He was a man all right. His strong thighs pumped as he strode up the hill under the well-cut jeans. She couldn't tell his age because of the shade thrown over his face by the broad-brimmed black Akubra, but he was fit. Rampantly fit. She gulped.

Of course, that was judging by the speed he covered the distance between them—and the way the sun shone off his muscles below the shoulders of his sleeveless shirt. She tried to dredge up some saliva in her mouth and her heart felt as if it was beating as fast as Benson's. She could almost feel the testosterone from here. How come men in the city didn't shout about their maleness like this guy did?

At least he stopped at the bottom of the verandah steps. That gave her time to swallow again. The dark bristles of five-o'clock shadow glinted on his chin while a faint drift of soap assured her he bathed. She smiled to herself at the normality of soap and her shoulders relaxed a little. He was human.

Savannah remoistened her lips. 'Good afternoon. Can I help you?'

He lifted his hat and raked springy chocolate-brown hair back off his forehead. His eyes were dark blue and really quite beautiful. She lost the plot for a moment as she was drawn into them. Benson squirmed in her arms, trying to bury his head further under her arm. It helped bring her back to reality.

The man turned his hat in his hands and she wasn't sure if he was being polite or just letting his head breathe.

'Afternoon. You're Andy's niece?' His voice was deep and clear. A strong voice for a strong man. She supposed she'd expected a slow drawl. She suppressed a shiver of awareness.

'Savannah Laine. And you are?'

'Theo.' She knew that name and her shoulders relaxed a fraction. The country solicitor had said he'd arranged for Theo to care for the stock until she could come. She'd imagined a crusty old farmer. Well, he looked like a farmer but there was certainly no crust—and he wasn't old either!

'The gentleman who's been looking after the animals? Thank you for that.'

'No problem. Your uncle was a great guy.' His statement seemed genuine but his gaze held no hint of sympathy for her. It stiffened her spine.

'Yes, I know.' She ignored the prickle of tears in her eyes and changed the subject. 'The animals. That was my next job. So how many animals are there?'

He raised thick brown brows at her ignorance. 'In the pig shed there's six sows, a boar and a dozen or so growers that need to go to market soon. I'll come down with you and run you through the feed schedule board tonight, if you like.'

That many! Savannah swallowed.

He went on. 'There are twenty or so fowls. If you want to sell any eggs put them in a carton in your mail box and the mailman will leave you two dollars. And there's one rooster, but I'd be knocking him on the head. He's a pain.'

Savannah tried to imagine herself knocking a rooster on the head—what did you use? A hammer? She shuddered. 'He's probably safe for the moment.'

Theo gave a short laugh and it changed his face into something less harsh.

Thank goodness for that. For a while there she'd thought he was the frozen man. His eyes warmed in

genuine amusement and became even more mesmer-
ising until they went cold again. She dragged her attention back to what he was saying.

'Then there are the cattle—twenty Murray Grey
breeders, a placid Murray Grey bull and fifteen veal-
ers.'

She'd helped her uncle with the farm animals over
many holidays—she wasn't scared or lacking in confidence—but that was a heck of a lot of lives de-
pending on her.

'That's all?'

'Just Billy the horse and a couple of ducks and
geese, but they're pretty self-sufficient.'

Savannah nodded and tried to look nonchalant. 'If
you're not in a hurry, I could come down and see the
pigs with you now. What time do they normally eat?'
She put Benson down and descended the stairs to the
boot rack.

Theo looked at Benson cringing and quivering on
the verandah. He shook his head in disgust. Savannah
thought she heard him say 'Dishmop' but couldn't be
sure.

He looked at his watch. 'I've been coming around
about five in the afternoon and eight in the morning,
but they're pretty flexible. If you leave them too long,
they'll let you know.'

Savannah tapped the wellingtons upside down on
the ground and slipped one foot into her uncle's gumboots.

Theo was much taller than she was and she could
feel him looking down at her.

His voice was serious. 'I had a green tree snake in

one boot and a red-back spider in the other one yesterday.'

Savannah's foot hovered over the second boot. Had she checked it well enough?

She heard him snort and glared up at him. 'Very funny.'

His face was deadpan. 'So you reckon you can run this farm on your own?'

That snapped her head up. 'Why? Do you think I can't?'

He stared at her for a moment as if she'd really offended him, his eyes narrowed. Then he shook his head once. 'Lady, luckily, it's not my problem.' He turned and started to walk down the driveway to the sheds.

Macho moron. Savannah glared at the muscles of his back moulded against his shirt and clumped behind him in her uncle's big boots. She'd have to get herself a pair she didn't swim around in. She awkwardly skipped a couple of steps to make up some ground. Where had he learnt his social graces? The guy was a pain.

She almost laughed out loud when she remembered the rooster and what could happen to 'pains' around here. Theo probably wouldn't notice if she hit him on the head with a hammer.

She caught up with him as they crossed the dirt road and entered the bottom paddock together. Savannah tried not to get her boots stuck between the rails of the cattle grid as she crossed, but it felt like there was a magnet drawing her into the broken spaces. The sheds were old but, thank goodness, made

of thick hardwood planks that looked as if they'd still
be standing if she had grandchildren one day.

It hit her then that she was the sole person responsible for a two-hundred-acre farm, a two-bedroom
farmhouse and this menagerie of animals. She swallowed but Theo was getting away while she thought
about it and she had to skip a couple more steps.

The pigs heard their approach and started to squeal
and shriek in excitement. The thick smell of happy
pigs cloyed the air but Savannah didn't mind it.

It made her think of an uncle who'd paid her fifty
cents per sty to hose them out, and had then taken
her to the local show to spend the money. She could
almost feel the tickle and taste of the fairyfloss they'd
bought.

She followed Theo into the old office and stopped
in front of the whiteboard nailed to the wall. Each
pig's name had a number next to it for the amount of
pails of food it needed.

'Bruce is the boar, I gather?' She looked sideways
at Theo. 'So how come he gets three pails and Rosa
only gets one and a half?'

'Bruce has six women vying for his attention. He
has to keep up his strength, poor guy. I couldn't think
of anything worse.'

'Ah. A woman-hater. Personally, I feel sorry for
Rosa and the other girls. He probably doesn't shave.'

Why had she said that? She felt the rush of heat
up her face but he didn't even look at her.

'They're happy enough if you meet their material
needs.'

I'll bet there's a story in that, she thought, but prudently restrained herself.

Theo had started instructing. 'The pig pellets are in this drum. Make sure you put the brick back on top of the lid or the rats get trapped in there and jump out at you when you open it next.'

Savannah winced. That was one task she wouldn't forget to do.

'The pig's water is piped to those drinking nipples at the side of each pen. You check the nipple as you feed to see if they're working. The water is pumped from the river so you won't run out.'

He looked at her from under his frown. 'I hosed the concrete pens out early this morning but you need to do them at least every two days.'

'My uncle usually did them daily and I'll do the same.'

He grunted, looked at her as if to say 'yeah, sure', but didn't comment. They walked the length of the big shed, doling out pails of feed from the bucket he'd filled and checking the water nipples. He stopped beside the last pen. 'Louise's litter is due in the next week. She should be fine.'

Savannah had had just about enough of his condescending looks. 'I have my midwifery certificate, so I'm sure we'll manage.'

His face twitched, then he smiled, and then he chuckled. It was deep and rumbly and infectious.

Savannah couldn't help her own smile as she watched him in surprise. He threw back his head and she stared at the strong column of his throat as he laughed.

He wiped his eyes and dragged himself under control. And looked almost as surprised at himself as she was. 'I'm sorry, it's the thought of you telling the sow to breathe while you catch the piglets.' His expression straightened. 'I'd love to be a fly on the wall.'

His cheekbones were high and his lips were more sexy than sculpted. She wondered what those bristles would feel like against her face.

This was getting crazy. 'Well, there seem to be a few flies already on the wall here, and I think that's everybody fed. I need to meet the chickens.'

You coward, Savannah, she chided herself, but it was good to feel the breeze on her hot cheeks once they were outside the shed—and not just because of the smell.

They collected the eggs and he showed her the feed tin and how much to give. None of the cows were being milked so that was one chore she didn't have to worry about.

She supposed it would be polite to offer him a drink for his help. But was it safe? She decided to take the risk. 'Would you like a cup of tea?'

'No, thanks. I'll be going if you haven't any more questions.' He tipped his hat and presented her with his gorgeous back and taut backside as he walked away. Watching him, it made her want to sign up at a gym, although at least living this far out of town she was safe from that. She had a mental picture of herself working out in gumboots and smiled.

Theo certainly wasn't a talkative blighter and was obviously not going to be an intrusive neighbour. The strange thing was her own disappointment because he didn't want to stay.

Savannah clumped back up the driveway to the house. She decided against more unpacking and went to shower in the soft rainwater from the tank.

When she was finished, she stood in the steamy bathroom and her towel stilled as she remembered the impact Theo had made on her as he'd laughed in the shed. And even before that. She had to admit she couldn't remember a more arresting man.

Unfortunately he made her think of barns and hay and dappled sunlight and naked skin on naked skin. It was as if Theo had found and activated her erotic thought button—which was funny because Greg hadn't discovered it in the two years she'd lived with him.

She jammed the towel through the rail and shivered despite the sudden flush of heat that had invaded her body. Deal with it. She didn't need to complicate her life with a man. Especially a sinfully physical one with attitude.

This was her chance to be herself. Not trying to be the person someone else thought she was. Not expecting anything from anyone. First her mother and then her ex-fiancé Greg had hurt her—letting her assume his wife was completely out of the picture. From now on she would rely only on herself. She *could* do this. She *could* run this farm, start work next week at the small local hospital and live a full life. Be happy as she hadn't been since the times she'd spent here.

As she glanced around the spartan room the memories crowded her mind. Memories of days filled with laughter, her uncle's booming voice and, way back in the past, her aunt's quieter tones that had conveyed so much warmth. Savannah was the child they'd never had and they had been the parents she'd wished had been hers.

Even after her aunt had died, her uncle had still encouraged her to come. He'd called it her crazy place where she could be the child she couldn't be when she lived at home with her widowed mother. A place to do silly things, like trying to ride a calf, climb trees or cuddle a piglet.

She remembered catching baby turtles in the creek with Dory, the older boy down the road. He'd seemed like a god to her with his long dark hair and broad shoulders. He'd left her tongue-tied one minute and feeling woman-wiser than him the next.

When she was fourteen, it was here she'd received her first kiss and fallen in love with the first boy who hadn't loved her back. She could still remember the devastation. Her loyal uncle had dried her tears and had vowed Dory had no taste.

The sadness welled up for a moment at her uncle's passing, and she felt herself stiffen to hold it in. Then she loosened her shoulders. She was home, after all. She could cry if she wanted to.

Savannah wiped the moisture from her eyes and sniffed. Her uncle had always been so proud of her. If only he'd told her he was sick, she would have come to help him even if Greg had objected. But it was too late now.

She crossed the bathroom, and opened the window

to let in the fresh air. She was *not* going to think about Greg. From now on she was her own woman and this was a new life. She couldn't wait to start work next week!

'And this is our resident doctor, Dr McWilliam, whom we mentioned at the interview.'

The stillness in Savannah's face wasn't because the old-fashioned waiting room in Bendbrook Hospital was empty and she was used to being in charge of a busy emergency department in one of Sydney's largest hospitals. It wasn't even the waves of hostility she felt emanating from Julia West, the now second-in-charge nurse showing her the ward. It was the blow to her solar plexus delivered by a pair of beautiful blue eyes creased at the corners and the broad shoulders of a man she'd already met.

'So our new leader arrives. Hello, Savannah.' There was no warmth in Theo's voice.

Savannah worked frantically to correct the tilt in her world's axis. McWilliam. So Theo would be Theodore. *Dory.* Dory McWilliam. My God!

She'd thought he would have moved or married or something. She hadn't even recognised him. He seemed different to the man she'd met last week but if she looked hard she could see traces of the boy beneath the man. He'd been an arrogant teenager then—but she'd still fallen for him—and it didn't look like he'd changed.

He was neat and tidy, his face was shaved—it had been a crime to hide that jaw—and his thick brown hair was now cut close to his head. He still looked incredibly sexy and she felt his impact right down to her toes. Dory McWilliam.

A metamorphosis from the boy she remembered, and she wondered what sort of a doctor he was. She'd bet he kissed differently now!

Now, that was unprofessional. Stop it!

She ignored the warmth of her cheeks, held out her hand and then instantly regretted it. Her fingers were taken, squeezed and probably left incapable of feeling anything but his touch for the next hour—and this was only the first time she'd actually touched him in fifteen years. Yep. She was in trouble!

Luckily she had her voice under control. 'So you're Dr McWilliam. I think I met a relative of yours a few days ago.'

'That would be the one on holidays.' He nodded.

'Hmm. It's pleasant to meet you, too.' Actually, she was thinking, thanks for ruining my life. She'd moved from Sydney to break her chronic habit of falling for the wrong man but it seemed she'd turned full circle. Well, this could be her third chance—she'd work on a cure this time.

She forced herself to move away from him and get on with her day. It seemed a positive diversional tactic. 'Thank you for introducing me to everyone, Julia. We should have a good morning.'

'If you say so.' Julia West was tall, willowy, dressed in the plain blue sister's uniform and clearly unamused at being passed over for the top job.

Savannah gave her a sunny smile. 'We'll certainly work on it.' She slid her bag into the spare cupboard under the desk and slipped the key into her pocket.

At least she'd had some orientation and knew where most things were and went. It didn't look like sweet Julia was going to be particularly helpful today. But as long as it didn't affect the quality of care for their patients, she was entitled to it.

The sound of the first ambulance of the day drew her attention and both women walked to the emergency entrance to greet it.

Theo drained his coffee-cup, threw his stethoscope around his neck and stood up to stretch. With less than two hours of the sixteen-hour night shift to work, he was feeling remarkably awake.

In fact, he was feeling more awake than he'd felt for the last two years since he'd moved back here. Of course, he'd just had a month's break from work, and despite the frustration and disappointment with Sam's cancelled visit, there was novelty in change.

He grunted. Change was usually a stimulant—it had nothing to do with his new neighbour who was poured so deliciously into her floral administration uniform.

His thoughts had persistently wandered to Savannah over the weekend but he'd resisted the urge to check on her.

He'd even convinced himself she'd probably have a few disasters, although hopefully all the animals would survive. Then she'd give up and shift back to the city she'd come from. And he could ignore the shock of attraction he'd tried to forget when he'd seen her for the first time in fifteen years.

She'd come for holidays when she'd been younger, like a black-haired Madonna with her serious face.

Those dark violet eyes of hers had seemed to see right through him.

Her hair had been long then, but he liked the way it curled around her face and bounced out now, like those Patty Duke movies his mother had loved to watch.

She'd certainly grown up. Unfortunately, it wasn't just her luscious little body that grabbed his attention. There were memories, too.

Theo remembered the direct look she'd given him the first time he'd kissed her all those years ago. As if to say, So that's what it's all about.

When he'd found out the name of the new charge sister for the emergency department, he'd flinched and realised there were two places he had to avoid Savannah now. He'd completely forgotten that Andy had spoken of his niece being a nurse.

Of all the bad luck.

CHAPTER TWO

THEO needed to stay focused on his own agenda. Savannah Laine could not be allowed to affect his life.

Julia was on her way back to the office and he raised his eyebrows.

'Ready for me yet?'

'Yes.' She slid open the filing-cabinet drawer and withdrew some patient notes. 'You remember Mrs Reddy?'

'Elsie with emphysema.' He held his hand out for the old medical records.

'That's right. She was too breathless to stay home. Savannah…' she rolled her eyes '…is settling her in.'

'I'll be there in a minute. I'll have a quick look at her usual medications first.'

'My, you're eager for work this morning. How strange,' she said over her shoulder as she walked away. 'I'll go and put the coffee-jug on as no one needs me.'

What was wrong with Julia? She wasn't usually this moody. Theo frowned at her back and flicked through the patient's notes.

Elsie Reddy. Last admission a month ago, also for breathlessness.

She'd been given home oxygen, a Ventolin nebuliser, fluid tablets, potassium supplement to replace

24

what the fluid tablet took out, digoxin for heart rhythm, quinine for leg cramps—all the usuals.

He particularly remembered that she had bad veins for getting blood. But it was time for a look. He walked onto the ward.

'Good morning, Mrs Reddy. I'm Dr McWilliam.'

'I know.' Elsie Reddy's face was pale except for two spots of unhealthy colour in her cheeks, but the soft wheezing voice still held a smile. 'Big virile man like an out-of-work stuntman.' She took a breath. 'Got yourself a woman yet?' She laboured to catch her breath again.

Theo looked at Savannah who was standing by the old lady's bed, and glared at the suppressed amusement he saw in her face. He looked back at the older woman. 'How about you try to not talk and I'll have a listen to your chest?'

'When I'm not talking I'll be dead,' she said, but sank wearily back against the high pillows and closed her eyes.

Savannah smiled at the old lady's dry comment. 'Mrs Reddy's temperature isn't elevated but it's pretty cold outside this morning. Her respirations are thirty-two and blood pressure's up.'

'You think she's got an infection?' He raised his head and looked at Savannah. When she nodded her hair bounced. He frowned and concentrated. 'I'll put a line in, get some blood gas analysis from Pathology and we'll start some Ventolin via nebuliser and maybe antibiotics later.'

They both heard the sound of another ambulance pulling up outside.

Savannah tilted her head. 'Leave me a quick written order and I'll put the cannula in and get a Ventolin nebuliser going while you see to that one.'

Theo raised his eyebrows. *'You'll* put the cannula in? The winds of change are obviously blowing.' He shrugged. 'But that'll certainly make my job easier.' He scribbled on the notes, patted Mrs Reddy's arm and left.

Savannah smiled at the old lady. 'Did you catch all that?'

'Most of it.'

'I'll pop a drip in this arm, take some blood, then we'll put something into the bag of fluid to help your lungs work better.'

'My veins are bad.' The memories of past jabs shone in wary eyes.

Savannah lifted the frail arm and ran her fingers lightly over the papery skin. 'Yours look better than the veins they've been showing me in the city lately.'

Five minutes later, Theo poked his head around the curtain. Savannah was cleaning up after completing the tasks quickly and competently.

He nodded. 'I'm impressed. Can I borrow you?'

She barely glanced at him. 'Sure, but check these ampoules first, please, and I'll start this infusion.'

'Bossy little thing, aren't you?' She certainly hadn't been bossy fifteen years ago and Theo wasn't quite sure he appreciated her lack of deference now!

She raised her own eyebrows and this time met his eyes. 'You have no idea.'

Savannah turned back to her patient and lifted the mask over Elsie's face, then slid the nurse-call button into her hand. 'Ring me if you're worried, but you should start to feel better soon. I'll be back as quick as I can.'

Theo watched her gentleness with the old lady and forgave her assertiveness. He sighed. He'd probably have to get used to it.

The sound of another ambulance, this one with the siren wailing, made Savannah and Theo look at each other. 'The all-or-nothing law of country hospitals,' he said with resignation. They moved towards the entrance.

Savannah shrugged. 'Well, the city ones don't have a quiet time except maybe at four o'clock on a Sunday morning—so we'll manage.'

The new patient had all their attention after one glance.

The ambulance officer passed the history over quickly. 'Mr Grey was found almost unconscious under his house. He'd been doing some dusting for fleas.'

The white-haired man on the stretcher was pale and saturated with sweat. His nose was running and his chest gurgled with fluid. Savannah felt the leap in her own pulse rate at the sight of the gravely ill man.

His clothes were covered with a fine powder and he lay limp on the trolley except for the twitches he had no control over.

'Wear some gloves and get his clothes off. Looks like organophosphate poisoning.'

Savannah did a double-take. This was a different Theo. This doctor was fast, sure and determined to keep his patient alive until the intravenous line he'd quickly inserted could be used to inject the atropine he was drawing up. They had a chance.

Savannah snatched a pair of disposable gloves from the box and started to strip the shorts and T-shirt from the man.

''It's a parasympathetic nervous system reaction from the pesticides, isn't it?' she asked quietly.

'Right. Not wearing full-length clothes wouldn't help. The poison is absorbed through the lungs, gut and skin. So until you get his skin washed he's still absorbing the poison into his system. All I can do is keep giving atropine, which has the opposite effect on the body. Hopefully it will override his nervous system response, which is to produce so much in the way of secretions he could drown in them.'

The man was gasping for breath and Savannah could well believe Theo's worst-case scenario. Savannah swiftly applied the cardiac leads and began to sponge the man's body. Julia arrived to help and kept replacing the water dish and washers with fresh ones.

'Pinpoint pupils and respirations are faster and shallower.' Savannah dried him and pulled a warm blanket over his twitching body. Her voice was steady. 'Blood pressure's falling, he looks like he might fit.'

Theo was calm but intense. 'Pump the intravenous fluid into his veins—it's hypovolaemic shock from the fluid shift. Pupils are beginning to dilate so the atropine is starting to take effect. He should improve soon. It's usually quite dramatic. Looks like they got him here just in time.' They both glanced at the monitors and nodded.

'Vital signs are stabilising, and his twitching has decreased. Stop pumping the fluid in and we'll just run it normally now.' Savannah removed her hand from the manual pump bulb on the IV line and flexed her fingers.

That had been close. Any doubts she'd had about Theo's skill were gone.

Theo was looking down at the patient when the man opened his eyes.

'Hello, old son.' He squeezed the man's shoulder and Savannah blinked at the kindness in Theo's eyes. 'You gave us a scare for a while there. You should be on the mend now but we need to move you up to Intensive Care for at least seventy-two hours.' He turned away to write up the notes on Mr Grey. 'Speed his transfer to the unit, Sister. I'll go out and see his wife.'

Two broken legs, a toddler with a temperature and a teenage boy's three-day-old burn that needed redressing saw them through to morning tea.

Theo was off home at ten, Mrs Reddy and the two orthopaedic patients had been transferred to the wards and the toddler sent home with a script. Savannah looked around. The ward was back to empty.

'That was fun.' Theo's voice was dry and he met Savannah's eyes. They froze for a moment before both turned away. He felt like a cruising jock in high school and the feeling was so alien to him he shook his head.

Must be sleep deprivation, he decided. He hadn't felt like this for years!

He stretched before he patted his pocket for his keys. 'Well, it's been interesting, working with you. I'm back on the ten-to-six day shift tomorrow so I'll see you then.'

Savannah tried not to stare at his broad back and neat denim-clad bottom as he strolled out the door. She mentally kicked herself. He turned and saluted Julia who was on her way back to the desk after restocking a trolley.

Savannah forced her eyes away from Theo's departing figure. 'He seems very competent and caring with the patients,' she commented.

Julia's eyebrows were raised. 'Hmm. He's quick but thorough, not like some around here. Plus he's not hard on the eyes—especially with his hair cut. But the ex-wife soured him and he's emotionally dead.' There was bitterness in Julia's voice that spoke of an unsatisfactory love life of her own. Savannah met her eyes.

'That's OK, I'm trying for celibacy,' she replied, and was pleasantly surprised when Julia gave a short laugh. There was hope for her yet!

Julia looked up, curious. 'So how do you two know each other?'

'I met him one day last week. He lives on the nearest property and looked after my late uncle's farm until I moved up here. We actually played together as kids when I came up for holidays, but I don't think he remembers.'

Julia nodded. 'I'm sorry to hear about your uncle.

And I was less than welcoming this morning. Ask me anything about the place.'

'We'll take it slow. I'm not going to rush in and change everything, but if I can see something that makes our job easier and more efficient, we can look into it. Obviously the computer age hasn't caught up with Bendbrook yet so that's on my list.' Savannah glanced at the clock. 'Where's the doctor that starts at ten?'

'One of our local GPs, Dr Hudson—' that hint of bitterness again laced Julia's voice '—does the odd shift when we can't get a resident. He usually runs late.'

'What if an emergency comes in?'

'Theo has breakfast at the canteen before he goes to bed. We call him back if we're desperate. In that respect we're really lucky to have him. We've had some less-than-perfect residents. The medical super-intendent tried to get Theo to sign a contract—they even offered him the post of Director of Emergency—but he says he's not interested. Refuses to be tied down.'

One of those. Savannah decided it was time to stop discussing Dr McWilliam and filed away the issue of tardy Dr Hudson for a discussion on punctuality later. 'Let's have a look at this stock order.'

The canteen was quiet and Theo was giving himself a harsh talking-to. He was getting involved. He'd not looked at another woman since Marie had ground him into the dust, and he wasn't going to start now. You couldn't trust them. So many times he'd thought he'd

won custody of Sam and then Marie had pulled something else out of the hat. He'd finally realised she
enjoyed his pain.

He didn't know how much more he could take. His
life was marking time until he could win custody of
Sam, and his lawyer promised that day would soon
come.

Theo didn't want to complicate it with an overly
demanding job—he had to be free to be able to leave
at any minute if needed. But what about Andy's
niece?

Savannah provoked a response in him that he didn't
understand. She was bossy, and yet caring with her
patients. There was something about her that pierced
his usual wall of indifference that protected him from
the female of the species.

Maybe if he found out what it was he could inoc-
ulate himself against her like a flu vaccine. He forked
the last of his powdered scrambled eggs into his
mouth and swallowed it with a grimace. He needed
to get home and out of here.

The pigs were cross. Their mistress had not seen them
all day and had then decided to change her sty-
cleaning time to before the evening meal. They
squealed, nudged and butted her legs as she hosed,
but she refused to give in until the floor was clean.

'It's OK, you girls. I'll feed you soon. Anyone
would think you hadn't eaten for a week.'

Bruce stared with piggy eyes through the slats in
his own clean pen and grunted and munched.

Savannah smiled as she hosed. They were all characters. Rachel was bossy, Hilda a greedy guts and Trisha was timid. Rosa and Keira looked exactly the same and she called them the twins.

Poor old Louise was ponderous with her unborn babies and Savannah kept telling herself a pig could have piglets without a human's help.

It had been too cold to clean the sties before work and surprisingly she found it mindlessly relaxing after the tension of starting the new job that day. And recognising the first boy she'd ever kissed. It was crazy. They'd been kids. It meant nothing.

The sound of water hitting concrete and the cacophony of the pigs masked Theo's approach.

He leaned back against the debarked tree-trunk used as the centre pole of the pig shed and watched her as she talked to the pigs.

She looked younger in a man's flannelette shirt with sleeves rolled up and a pair of old jeans tucked into Andy's boots. She'd certainly filled out and gained confidence over the years. He'd found that out at work.

One of the sows butted her in her nicely rounded backside and she barely flinched as she turned the hose on the offender with a laugh. He had to admit it, she handled the animals well.

Now that he looked, he could see a glimpse of the girl from the past. Especially when she laughed. She'd had that same bubbly chuckle all those years ago. He'd teased her about it. But on the rare occasions he'd heard it then, and listening now, it still made him smile.

He wasn't even sure why he was here. He'd had

trouble sleeping today and once it had hit four o'clock he hadn't been able to stay in bed any longer.

He told himself he was being neighbourly, checking on her for Andy's sake, but he wasn't quite convincing himself.

She'd been so competent at work that morning that he wondered if he'd secretly hoped she'd look at a loss on the farm. He could despise a city slicker like his ex-wife.

No such luck. But he couldn't afford to get sidetracked here.

Sam was the major factor in his life and always would be. He wasn't free to dally for the fun of it. But there was something about her...

Savannah released the trigger on the hose and tipped the last of the pellets onto the floor of the final pen.

The noise level went from screaming pitch to munching level in the space of two seconds. She laughed out loud.

Theo took his shoulder off the pole. 'If only everyone were that easy to please.'

Savannah jumped at the sound of Theo's voice and spun to face him. Unconsciously she aimed the hose at his chest and he raised his hands.

CHAPTER THREE

'DON'T shoot.'

'Well, don't sneak up on me!'

Savannah lowered the hose and Theo put his hands down. His lips twitched at her threatening attitude.

'A brass band could sneak up on you with the noise this lot makes. Where's your guard dog?'

'Benson doesn't like the pigs. He's asleep up at the house.' Savannah collected the empty buckets and pails and passed him to go into the office.

He followed her. He didn't understand it. 'Why do you have a dog like that?'

'He was my mother's.'

A strange, vulnerable look crossed her face and it looked out of place on the confident woman he'd met twice. 'I'm sorry, has something happened to your mother?'

'Yes. She tired of the dog. Like she tires of everything. So I took him.'

This was too deep for him. He didn't want to know why she hurt when he asked about the dog.

Savannah could see he looked uncomfortable. She turned and walked towards the driveway. 'Did you want something, Theo?'

'No. I was just checking that you were getting on all right with the animals, and I've brought my phone number in case you need help with an emergency on the farm.' He handed her a piece of cardboard he'd ripped off a cereal box.

'That's very thoughtful of you. Thank you.' She grinned at the brand. 'Coco Pops? I hadn't picked you as a chocolate-covered-cereal-eater, Theo.'

'They were for a guest who never came.' He looked away and changed the subject. 'Tell me how the rest of your first day at work went then I'll push off.'

'It was fine. There are a few areas I think we could streamline, and I'd love your input.' She saw the look on his face. 'If you're interested?'

His face remained closed. 'In discussing improvements? Not really. I do my shift and go home. I'll leave all that to the enthusiastic ones like you.'

Savannah narrowed her eyes. The guy was a selfish jerk. How could a health professional not be interested in the smooth running of the department? She supposed it went along with the man who wouldn't accept a permanent job.

She had to stop expecting people to be things they weren't. She should have learnt with her mother—and Greg. 'Then you'll have to excuse me. I'm looking forward to my shower.'

He screwed up his nose. 'You need one.' He spun right as they crossed the road and headed down it towards his own home a couple of bends further up the road.

She spoke to his retreating back. 'I'm not ashamed of it. Honest labour dirties your hands, Theo.'

He didn't answer.

Savannah steamed all the way up the driveway.

Mainly because she was ashamed of her rudeness to him. Sixteen hours of night shift *was* honest labour. And he'd come to check she was OK and bring his phone number in case she needed him. She was the jerk. But that crack about her needing a shower had been petty. She sniffed her sleeve and screwed up her nose. 'Phew.' Maybe more truthful than petty after all!

She kicked her boots off at the bottom of the stairs and stomped onto the verandah. She wasn't normally this short-tempered or intolerant. Perhaps she had more of her mother in her than she'd thought. Ouch. She preferred to believe it was because she hadn't slept well the night before. Without the sounds of the traffic in the city she'd found it difficult to settle, and the old house creaked and groaned a lot. Or maybe she was scared because she was impossibly attracted to Theo and he was just as prickly as she was.

Benson yapped from inside the house.

'Ha. Guard dog indeed! Where were you when I needed you?'

The next morning Savannah planned to apologise to Theo as soon as he came in. But she didn't have time.

Dr Smythe, a thin, nervous man, slow to work with and easily flustered, had patients banked back to the doorway. He'd spent nearly an hour trying to put a drip in a young man who had accidentally chainsawed a zipper in his leg, and in the end Savannah had tact-fully offered to do it herself.

By the time Theo arrived, Savannah was ready to throw her arms around him. He raised his eyebrows at the pile of waiting patient cards, and looked at her sardonically.

'Smythe snowed under, is he?'

'Yes,' Savannah said with great restraint.

'Well, let's get moving, then.'

Savannah heaved a sigh of relief and followed him from cubicle to cubicle. She watched, impressed, as he soothed frayed nerves and anxious relatives made worse by the long wait. He remained even-tempered and very thorough. He was very good at his job. Why wouldn't he take it on permanently?

By the time lunchtime came she was ready for a break. But she didn't get one.

'Savannah. In here, please.' The urgent summons from Julia in cubicle three had all thoughts of food banished immediately.

The very young woman behind the curtain was large all over and shapeless in a thick jumper. Tears rolled down her cheek and there was real fear in her eyes.

'Let me go to the toilet. I've got to go.'

Savannah took one look at the ungainly woman struggling to sit up and remembered another large young woman from her previous hospital whom she'd never forget.

'Can you hang on for one more minute while Sister fills me in?' Savannah looked at Julia.

'This is Carly, she's fifteen. I can't get much of a history but wondered if she had an acute appendicitis, except the pain comes and goes.'

'I'll bet. Carly, let me have a very quick feel of your tummy, and then we'll talk about your pain.'

Savannah lifted the baggy jumper and shirt underneath and ran her hands over the girl's round but not
bulging stomach. She felt a definite kick from the
baby within. The top of the uterus was palpable as
being consistent with a full-term baby. She caught
Julia's eye and nodded at the incredulous look on her
face.

'Get her a trolley and over to Maternity Ward, and
ring to say we're coming. She's ready to…' Savannah
stopped and sought another way to say it. 'Be transferred. Ask Theo to come in, please.'

Julia scooted out the door. Carly was between con-
tractions at the moment and Savannah needed some
information. She might have two minutes before the
next one.

'Carly, have you been to see a doctor in the last
year?'

'No.'

'Where's your mum?'

'She's in the waiting room with Dad.'

'Are you bleeding down below?' Savannah was
aware of Theo's feet stopping outside the curtain. The
curtain parted slightly and his eyes met hers. She held
her finger up for a second and he stood back.
Savannah looked back at the girl.

A pink flush rose in her cheeks and the girl looked
away. 'I think I might have my period, but I only
ever had one so I'm not sure.' Baby blue eyes looked
up at Savannah with relief. 'So that's why I have
pains. It's a period.'

'I don't think it's a period. Carly, I'm sorry to ask
you this, but are you a virgin?'

This time the cheeks stayed pink. There was a silence and Savannah willed the girl to answer before the next contraction.

Carly swallowed. 'I'm nearly a virgin. I only did it the once and that was a long time ago.'

'About nine months?' Savannah smiled softly down at the naïve young woman beside her.

Carly's lip quivered and she turned tear-filled eyes up at Savannah. 'I'm having a baby?' She sniffed. 'I really hoped I wasn't.'

Savannah reached for her hand. 'Very soon.'

Her eyes widened. 'I don't know how. Don't you have to go to classes or something to learn how to breathe?'

Savannah couldn't help the smile this time. 'No. Your body will let you know what to do. Don't be scared and just do what your body tells you.'

'Mum and Dad will kill me.' Her eyes widened and she groaned. 'My body's telling me I want to go to the toilet.' She squeezed her eyes shut, crushed Savannah's hand and grunted.

Theo stepped from behind the curtain and into the cubicle. 'I gather we're having an unplanned baby.'

'I was hoping we'd get her to Maternity first but she must have been in second stage when she came in.'

'How could you tell if you haven't examined her?'

Savannah gave him an old-fashioned look. 'Let's say my experience tells me.'

Savannah leaned her face close to the girl's and stroked her cheek. 'Carly, the doctor's here. It's OK, sweetheart. Do you want your mum?'

At the girl's tentative nod, Savannah straightened. 'What's her name?'

'Ruth.'

'I'll be back in a tick.'

Theo looked up. 'You're not leaving me here?'

'Yeah, wish I could be a fly on the wall.' She saw him frown and she smiled. 'I'll be quick.'

She closed the curtain and glanced up the corridor. The orderly was coming to push the bed to Maternity. With a bit of luck they might make it there yet. She picked up a prepackaged emergency delivery set and tucked the paper-covered bundle under her arm—description side down—just in case.

Savannah turned the other way into the waiting room. There were only two people left in there—a large-boned woman who could be none other than Carly's mum, and the other a thin, bald man turning his hat in his hands. Both stood up when Savannah entered.

Worried blue eyes searched Savannah's face. 'How's my Carly?'

'She'll be fine but she needs her mum. Can you follow me, please?'

Ruth touched her husband on the arm and gestured for him to take her handbag. 'What about her dad?'

'Perhaps it's better if he stayed here for the moment. He can come in if you want him, too, shortly. The cubicles are very small.'

They strode quickly back towards the cubicles. Ruth caught Savannah's arm. 'What's wrong with her?'

Savannah tried to imagine how she would feel as

a mother in this situation. Procrastination wouldn't help.

'Carly is having a baby.'

The breath puffed between Ruth's lips. 'When?'

'Today. Now.'

Ruth stopped walking, closed her eyes for a second and then started to walk again. 'Then we'll leave her father in the waiting room.'

Theo was sweating. He'd specialised in orthopaedics, not obstetrics. He had no doubt he could deliver a baby, despite the five years or so since the last one, but he had to make the decision to stay or go to Maternity. He didn't want this child, with no antenatal care, born in a corridor between the two wards.

What was keeping Savannah? He realised he missed her calmness. Just as he decided to go for Maternity, Carly put her chin on her chest and screamed. Well, that made the decision easy. Looked like it was here.

Savannah swished through the curtains and surprisingly she was smiling. She put an emergency delivery set-up on the bottom of the bed and started to open it. Good idea!

Carly's mum followed her. Ruth went straight to her daughter and kissed her.

'Duffer. You should have told me. Now, stop that screaming and give it a shove, like you gotta go.'

Theo met Savannah's eyes and both smiled. She mimed that he should go and wash his hands and waved a pair of gloves at him.

He felt the smile tugging on his lips and did as he

was told. How had Savannah turned this situation into normal so quickly?

In the few seconds he was gone, Savannah had Carly sit higher in the bed, slip her trackpants off and hold herself under her thighs with her hands. The sheet across her lap gave some degree of dignity. Her mother rested her arm around Carly's shoulders.

Theo marvelled as determination replaced the look of fear on the girl's face and a dark crescent of the baby's head protruded between her legs. He heard her gasp at the sensation. He winced. It was at moments like this he was glad he was a man.

Theo's hand hovered over the bulge of the baby's head, not touching but ready in case Carly decided to push without control. But she didn't. Incredible girl.

The back of the baby's dark head of hair continued to distend the vulva until it seemed there couldn't possibly be more room, and then the head started to extend as the baby lifted its chin inside its mother.

First the top of the head and then, centimetre by centimetre, the forehead swept the perineum until the gentle rush of nose, mouth and chin completed the first of the obstacles to the outside.

They all sighed. 'You're doing beautifully, Carly.' Theo's voice was quiet and didn't disturb the mood of the occasion.

'It's stinging, burning like mad.' Carly groaned between her teeth.

'It must be. Just relax for a moment until you get another contraction. I'm going to feel if the umbilical cord is around the baby's neck in case it's too tight.'

He slipped one finger next to the baby's neck and circled it. 'No cord.'

'I'm getting another pain.'

'Then push,' said her matter-of-fact mother.

First one shoulder was born for Theo to slip his finger into the axilla and then the other, and in a rush the body and legs followed. Theo lifted the child onto Carly's stomach by the baby's armpits and Savannah laid a small blanket across the pair to block out any breeze.

Ruth kissed her daughter and wiped the tears from her own cheek with the back of her hand.

Carly wasn't satisfied. 'Well, what is it?'

They all looked at each other and Savannah's eyes twinkled. She lifted the blanket again. Theo raised the child for Carly to say it first.

'It's a boy. Thank goodness. He doesn't have to go through that.'

They all laughed.

Soon third stage was complete, both mother and child had been checked over and Theo left to write up the notes.

Ruth brought in the new grandfather. He stood there, blinked, opened and closed his mouth a few times and then sank onto the only chair in the cubicle.

'Well?' His wife nudged him to encourage some comment.

The older man cleared his throat. 'Are you both well?'

Carly barely met her father's eyes as she nodded her head.

'That's good.' He sighed, stood up and leaned over

to kiss his daughter's cheek. 'Er, I always wanted a son. A grandson will be grand.'

Satisfied all would be well with her patient, Savannah slipped out to join Theo at the desk. He looked up with a straight face.

'Maternity rang and asked how come we did them out of their job?'

She smiled. The birth was a lovely memory to share. 'That was a nice delivery, Theo. Maybe you should work in obstetrics.'

He frowned.

Now what was wrong with him? She felt like kicking him out of the mood.

He shook his head. 'With no antenatal care, we're lucky the baby had no problems. I can't believe no one knew she was pregnant.'

'I think Carly had an idea, but hoped it would go away.'

He snorted. 'How?'

'If you were fifteen, scared and not sure what was going on, it might seem reasonable. Actually, I had a case exactly like Carly's at my last hospital—so it's not so unusual.' She tilted her head. 'Haven't you ever done something you regretted and wished the whole problem would go away?'

He froze and refused to meet her eyes. Man, had he! 'I'm going to the cafeteria for lunch. Ring me if you need me.'

Theo spent another meal talking to himself in the cafeteria. Savannah was right. Birth was special. Yet it was just another thing Marie had excluded him from. Maybe it was time he learned to deal with it.

Driving home that night, Theo forced himself not to slow down as he drove past Savannah's farm. Stopping by unexpectedly two days in a row would be too much.

CHAPTER FOUR

THE next day was Wednesday and Theo was a few minutes early for work.

The ward was quiet. There was a meeting being held in the staffroom, so Theo went along and leaned unobtrusively against the door of the room to watch Savannah in action. He'd spent a lot of time last night at home thinking about her and how she made him feel.

The problem was, he admired her. He had a feeling life had dealt her some hefty blows but she'd refused to go down.

She'd had a pretty rough childhood from what he could remember and there was a certain kinship in knowing everything hadn't been rosy for either of them.

He watched the animation in her face as she addressed the on- and off-duty staff from her ward. They all seemed to like her. She was discussing plans for improvements for the department and normally he would have wandered off by now.

He could tell when Savannah noticed him at the door because a tide of pink rose up her cheeks and he could almost feel her having to drag her thoughts back to what she was saying. So she was aware of him, too. He couldn't look away.

'I believe every registered nurse that works in this

department should have a cannulation certificate. How many times have you wished you could put the line in yourself when the doctor hasn't been available? In the city hospitals, registered nurses are doing it themselves. There's no reason you shouldn't be.'

Savannah looked around the half-dozen faces and Theo did, too. He could see there was some resistance to change, warring with a desire to provide good service.

Julia said, 'What's involved and who's going to let us practise on them?'

Savannah nodded. 'You're thinking practically. That's great. I'll get the learning package passed by the nursing side and through Dr Ross in the medical superintendent's office.'

Theo saw her sneak a look at him. She'd probably heard that Dr Ross thought the sun shone out of him, and if he supported her it would be a lot easier. He sighed. He'd told her he didn't want to get entangled in hospital politics.

Savannah continued, 'You'd start with the theory component and do the venipuncture certificate. One at a time, you follow the pathology technician for a couple of mornings and help take blood. Then when you're confident you can find even the difficult veins, the next step means you follow the residents and practise inserting cannulas. When the doctor is satisfied, you get assessed. If you pass, you do your own when necessary. If you don't pass, we go through it all again.'

Theo grimaced. Which doctors had she run this by? He didn't mind her having plans for improvement—

he just didn't want to get involved. She made him tired!

Julia was talking again. 'So we'd take blood as well. That would be handy for the weekends when the blood collector isn't on.'

'I do it anyway,' said one nurse.

'So do I,' said another.

'This is the point I want to make.' Savannah looked around again. She even seemed satisfied with their comments, until she caught sight of Theo's curled lip.

She narrowed her eyes at him and battle lines were drawn. He'd had enough and he straightened.

Savannah went on. 'Your skill in venipuncture isn't recognised formally or legally. Despite your good intentions, you're putting yourself at risk and that's not acceptable. This way, the hospital acknowledges your training and accepts responsibility if anything happens, like a needlestick injury.'

'That's true,' Julia said. 'But it's getting more scary with AIDS and hepatitis C. I'm not sure that I want to increase my chances of catching something by becoming accredited in venipuncture.'

Theo leaned back against the doorframe again.

'That's a good point,' Savannah answered. 'But because of the risks, are you going to stop giving intramuscular injections to your patients? We all work in an emergency department. How often do you get blood on you despite the gloves and the gowns? I believe that learning the correct technique in a formal learning package is going to increase your knowledge of safe practice across the board. We'll have the regional infection control officer come and talk to us about the latest information…'

Theo pushed himself off the door and walked away. He could hear Savannah's voice outlining the plans as he went. Her enthusiasm made him unsettled. He could remember a time when he would have revelled in the organisation and implementation of such a scheme.

But it was as if it had all drained out of him.

All he could think about was what Marie had done to him and Sam. The court had said the child was better off with his mother. Theo, as a single parent doing sixteen-hour shifts at the hospital, wouldn't have the time. They just couldn't see what Marie was really like—and that she was using Sam as a weapon against Theo.

He wondered what he could change to make the court see that his son would be better off with him. Maybe a stable relationship would help? But he could never get married again. Apart from the fact that no sane woman would take him on!

He didn't know many single women—except Julia and, of course, his new neighbour.

Sister Laine. Was a kiss—a decade and a half old—good enough reason to get married?

Savannah, following him down the corridor to the ward, saw Theo throw back his head and laugh out loud, and the lack of humour in the sound made her flinch. She walked up to touch him on the arm. 'Are you OK?'

He looked down at her and she recoiled from his eyes—so cold and hard. Then the look was gone.

'Did you want something, Savannah?' He raised one eyebrow.

She mistrusted his voice and his look and even considered dropping the whole thing until a better time. But it wasn't in her nature. What if there never was a better time? She held his eyes with hers. 'I've a couple of issues I'd like your help on, please, Theo.'

'Really.' The mobile eyebrow went up again. 'What would they be?'

'I noticed you caught some of the ward meeting and most of my idea about the cannulation course.' He looked away and her stomach sank. 'Will you help?'

He looked back, gave her a noncommittal grunt on her first point and raised his eyebrows. 'And the other "issue"?'

'I want your support for my submission to the medical superintendent for computer access in this department and for personal pagers or alarms for all the nursing staff who work in the department.'

'Now, that will cost money. I don't like your chances of that one, Sister.'

'Be serious, Theo. We need to have access to the latest information and treatments if we want to hold our own as an emergency department. That means computer access on tap. And as for pagers or alarms, I worked in a hospital where people were at risk of attack. It could happen here.' She brushed her fringe off her forehead.

'Sometimes there's only one staff member on this ward if the other is called away. I'm going to push for measures that provide my staff with greater safety, and I want your help.'

Theo shrugged. 'Good luck. I'm beginning to think if anyone can get it you can.'

She turned away to hide the fierceness she knew was on her face. He hadn't said no, and he was unaware how tenacious she was. She'd work on him.

The phone rang in the small office and Theo went in to pick it up. 'Emergency, Dr McWilliam.' He glanced at Savannah who'd gone in to pull out the roster book and start checking the staffing for shifts. She tried not to listen.

'Yes, damn her.'

Damn who? Savannah wondered if she should leave the room. She glanced across to see if he seemed to want her to leave and she saw him wince.

'No.' His voice was emphatic. Theo ran his fingers through his hair. 'I don't know. Let me think about this. I'll get back to you.'

She turned away again. It was too late to leave now. Theo put the phone down and stared into space.

She decided on one more try for his help before she left it for the day. 'So you'll discuss it with Dr Ross and support the ideas?'

'Hmm.' Whoever had made the phone call hadn't improved his humour.

Now he had something else on his mind and Savannah knew it. She sighed. There had to be a reason he was like this. What had happened to the man she believed was inside? She'd seen glimpses of the caring doctor. He wasn't as irresponsible as he made out and she wished she knew how to reach him. It was as if he'd built a wall of indifference for protection in case he became too involved. She'd leave it for the moment but he needn't think it was all going to go away.

'Fine' was all she said.

When Savannah went to see Dr Ross it was just as frustrating as talking to Theo. It was even harder to move the conversation around to the direction she wanted.

After extended pleasantries Savannah tried again.

'I would like to discuss some new strategies for streamlining the department, Dr Ross.'

'Of course you do, my dear.'

Savannah stifled her irritation at his patronising tone. She wondered what he'd say if she said, 'That's right old chap.'

He was off on his own agenda again. 'How are you going with the locums?' The bushy white eyebrows seemed constantly drawn together, even when he was smiling. She found it quite bizarre.

What had the question been? Right. 'Of the three I've seen, Dr McWilliam is very good in an emergency. But we need two more, specifically emergency department residents.'

'Theo is excellent. Maybe you could convince him to stay. Young fellow won't listen to me and I've been at him to settle down and take over as Director of Emergency.'

Savannah frowned, and tried to keep on track. 'You would be in a stronger position to ask him to stay than I would. And it still doesn't solve the lack of consistent standards of medical coverage. Dr McWilliam can't do it all.'

He shrugged without apology. 'I'm sure you realise how hard it is to find good doctors willing to work in the country.'

'I was thinking of doctors from other countries. We had some super Scottish residents at my last hospital.'

'Talk Theo into the director's job and I'll see what I can do about the new residents.' He looked at his watch. 'My! Look at the time.'

'If I could just mention the security concerns I have and the new computers?'

He stood up and extended his hand. 'Next time. Lovely chatting with you, dear. Keep up the good work.'

Savannah sighed and stood. The man was going to be sick of the sight of her by the time she was finished with him. She was patient but persistent. 'Can I make another appointment to see you to discuss the other issues I'm concerned about?'

'You could tell them to Theo and he could fill me in when he comes to see me, which would save you the time.'

'No, I'd like to. I don't begrudge the time. I'll see you soon.' Savannah smiled pleasantly and shook his hand.

By the time she'd walked back to the emergency department her feet were tapping less forcefully on the polished floors.

A bevy of crying children seemed to have descended on the unit and Julia shrugged her shoulders as she walked past, carrying a toddler with a bandaged foot. The phone in the office was ringing. Lucky she'd stomped back here quickly.

'Emergency. Sister Laine. Can I help you?'

'Yes. My ten-year-old daughter's been bitten on the arm by a red-back spider. I can't see much where she said it bit her and she said it's not hurting too badly at the moment. I thought they were poisonous? What should I do?'

'They are poisonous but less than one in five people bitten have major problems with red-back bites.' She reached for the information book on spider venom and tucked the phone under her chin while she looked it up. Damn the lack of computers at Bendbrook. At her Sydney hospital, the Internet was constantly used for updated information.

'Hold half an aspirin or some ice over the bite area and bring her in. Try and keep her from moving the arm. If you can catch the spider in a jar, that's helpful, but don't get bitten yourself.'

She repositioned the phone and her finger slid down the page. 'Here it is. It takes ten to forty minutes for the bite to become more painful—which is why I suggested the aspirin for a local anaesthetic to help her on the way in—and the pain may travel to under her arm. How far are you from the hospital?'

'Twenty minutes. Her name is Sally Roberts.'

'We'll be waiting for you, but drive carefully.'

'As long as I know she'll be all right until we get there, we'll be fine.'

'When you arrive, the doctor will decide if she needs antivenene or not—and we do have some if it's needed,' Savannah reassured the woman.

'Thanks. That's what I needed to know.'

'Can I just get a quick couple of details?' Savannah logged the call, hung up and transcribed what she'd recommended. She tucked the logbook under her arm and went to look for Theo, whom she found in the observation room. He was writing notes on an admission. She slid the sheet along the desk to make him aware of the admission to come.

Theo was impressed. 'Where did you hear about the aspirin?'

'At a conference on envenomation. I'm a mine of information on dangerous creatures.'

'Aren't you scared of spiders or snakes?'

'Not them, but I do have a thing about ants.'

He screwed his face up in disbelief. 'Ants? They're almost domestic.'

'Well, I'm not domestic and would prefer a snake any day.'

'I'm beginning to think you're a dangerous creature yourself.'

Savannah's face remained expressionless. 'You'd better believe it.' Well, she did finally feel out of her cage now she was away from her mother! She stared at all the full cubicles in the observation room. 'Where do you want me to start?'

He spun on the chair and ticked the cases off on his fingers. 'Eager for work. Great. Removal of sutures from hand on six-year-old in cubicle two, tetanus toxoid injection to twelve-year-old who sat on rusty nail in cubicle four, collect eye swab from three-week-old baby in cubicle six. Oh, and a coffee for exhausted doctor at desk.'

'You've had your morning tea. Sorry, I don't do coffee. But I can get the others.' She smiled sweetly.

Julia came past again, with an older baby on her hip this time.

'What is this, Julia? Children's day?' Savannah asked.

'Just coincidence with the number of kids, but this little lady's mummy left her bag in the shop and went back for it. She won't be long.'

'Give her to me while I gather up what I need.'

Julia passed across the round-eyed infant and Savannah cuddled her close. 'You gorgeous thing. Come with me while we wait for your mummy.'

The little one reminded her of Amelia. Greg's daughter had only been a little older than this child when Savannah had first met them. She missed the cuddles she'd showered on Amelia, and the joy she'd felt as part of a family threesome. She squeezed the baby once more. They probably didn't miss her.

Theo couldn't help watching Savannah with the child. Five minutes later he saw her hand over the baby to its mother with a fond kiss and then proceed to methodically clear the cubicles without a complaint from any of the treated children. He couldn't believe it. At least one of them should be protesting loudly!

'Hey, Pied Piper.'

Savannah looked up from solemnly delivering a jar holding three tiny black threads—the stitches she'd removed—to the six-year-old for showing to his dad.

'Are you talking to me, oh, Coffee King?'

He shook his head at her cheeky grin. 'Just wanted to say I'm impressed. You'll make a great mother.'

Her face changed and she walked away. 'Yes, I
would.'

Foot in mouth again. That was clearly a no-go
zone. Theo sighed. He couldn't remember the last
time he'd made a personal comment to someone at
work—he'd been that absorbed in his own problems.
Obviously it wasn't his forte.

Theo didn't have time to worry about it as the ten-
year-old girl with the suspected red-back spider bite
arrived. Savannah brought her straight through to
Observation for Theo to assess. She had two long
braids with yellow ribbons on them, but her expression didn't mirror the cheerful hair ornaments.

Her mother had captured the red-back, an
Australian species related to the black widow spider
group found worldwide. It had received its comeup-
pance and lay in the bottom of the jar, never to bite
again. The slash of red across its bulbous shiny black
body was definitive.

Sally's arm was red and the girl was holding it
gingerly. She was crying.

'My arm and my tummy hurts.'

Theo helped her climb on the bed. 'OK, Sally.
Sister will just take your blood pressure on the other
arm. And you look like you're working up a sweat
there. I'd say that nasty spider has given you a big
bite.'

He stepped aside for Savannah to get at Sally's arm
and examined the jar. He looked at Sally. 'I think he's
doing worse than you are, though.'

Sally sniffed and almost laughed. Theo turned to
the mother. 'Mrs Roberts, is it?'

The older woman wiped her work-roughened palm on her trousers and shook Theo's hand. 'Yes.'

'I'm Dr McWilliam. You've done a great job, bringing her in and catching the spider.' He smiled at her and the woman's eyes widened at his charm. She smiled back. Savannah could see Theo was oblivious to his effect on people when he dropped his distant demeanour.

It made her like him more.

He went on, 'Not all people who are bitten are given the antivenene but I think I'd like to see Sally has one of them as she's showing most of the symptoms of a decent bite. That means she has an injection now.'

Theo checked the bite site, which was swollen and red. 'That looks painful, Sally.' He squeezed her hand in sympathy. 'Unlike a lot of antivenenes there really has been very little allergic reaction to this type of antivenene, but we'd still like to keep her overnight after the injection.'

Mrs Roberts appeared confused. 'Sally's not allergic to anything that I know of.'

Savannah waved a pamphlet. 'There's always a slim chance she could have a reaction later on, though. I'll give you this pamphlet on signs of serum sickness that you would need to look out for over the next four to fourteen days.'

The mother still seemed anxious. 'What's serum sickness? I've heard of antivenene but never of serum sickness.'

Savannah looked at Theo and he gestured for her to continue. 'It's very rare and even less likely with the red-back antivenene, but involves a rash and flu-like symptoms. If anything like that happened you'd need to bring Sally back for us to check. But it's not a case of the cure being worse than the disease. The antivenene should relieve most of Sally's symptoms. Even the tummy pain is a common symptom of the bite.'

Theo wrote on the clipboard. 'Sister will give you an injection to make you feel better, Sally. Then she'll take you around to the children's ward for a sleep. I'll check up on you later. Mum can stay as long as she likes.'

'Thank you, Doctor.' Mrs Roberts shook Theo's hand. He grinned and gestured to Savannah.

'It looks like Sister is the spider expert.'

Savannah looked up. 'Especially black widows.' She smiled at him sweetly and then turned to Sally. 'I'll be back in a moment with the injection then we'll go around and see the children's ward staff.'

It was eight-thirty that evening and Savannah saw the headlights of a car shine in her front windows. She finished the sherry she'd been sipping and rose from the chair in front of the pot-bellied stove. Her dress-ing-gown was draped across the lounge and she grabbed it to slip on as she crossed the room.

As if she didn't unconsciously know who it was. She skittered away from that thought but couldn't help glancing in the mirror to check her hair. When she opened the door, Benson opened one eye, cocked an ear and started to yap.

'Who's a clever watchdog?' He wagged his short

curly tail in delight. 'Not you, goose. Go back to doggy dreams.'

Offended but resigned to ridicule, Benson trotted behind her out the door.

Savannah stepped onto the verandah, and leaned over the rail. It was Theo. She'd known whom but not why. He looked tall and broad, and a little tired.

'Good evening, Savannah.'

'Hello. On your way home? You're off late. I thought you finished at six?' It was good to see him. Unfortunately it came across too warmly in her voice.

He smiled and it wasn't fair—it stabbed her like a needle. And brought back ancient memories. Thank goodness he didn't smile at her like that at work. She'd spend half her time in a daze.

'I was in the canteen and got called back to deal with a minor RTA. Only a couple of broken ribs and a concussion, thankfully. Do you mind if I come in?' He looked unsure of his welcome, or maybe unsure of why he was here, and she wondered what he'd do if she said no. She didn't.

'Should I say, ' "Come in to my parlour,' said the spider to the fly"?'

He came up beside her on the steps and they walked along the verandah together. 'How about, "Come in because it's cold out here"?'

'It is chilly for late October. I've even put the fire on.'

Benson yapped and Savannah looked at the dog in surprise.

'You'd better make friends with my guard dog first or he'll rip your leg off.'

Theo bent down and Benson cringed. 'Hey, I won't hurt you.' He stroked the curly black hair on the dog's head. 'I'm sorry I called you a dishmop.' Benson wagged his tail once but that was it.

'Maybe you'll grow on him.'

Theo reached in front of her and opened the door to allow her to precede him. And she'd thought he had no manners.

'Am I growing on you?' His voice was right behind her ear and the room she'd thought was pleasantly warm became suddenly stifling. She stepped away a pace.

'Sit down.' She saw him look around and realised it was the first time he'd been here since her uncle had died. She'd softened the room with a few brightly coloured cushions and a vivid circular floor rug. And had moved all the furniture round.

She gestured to the chair she'd vacated not long ago and tilted her head. It was time to take control. Somehow he'd been directing the play since he'd arrived. She didn't know how he'd done it but it was time for a shift in the balance of power.

She sat on the lounge and tried to relax back into it. 'Can I offer you a drink? Sherry or wine?'

He rubbed his stomach. 'I'd better not. I haven't eaten yet.' He slanted a glance at her.

'Don't look at me. I'm no cook.'

His mouth tilted. 'So what do you eat?'

'Tins and take-aways. Benson doesn't complain.' What was he playing at? This was a different Theo again from the farmer and the efficient doctor.

He leaned back in the chair as if he was having no problem relaxing.

'I heard you say you weren't domestic, but I didn't believe it. You're obviously very good at running an emergency department, you've taken to animal husbandry like you were born to it, and you let a little thing like cooking beat you?'

Her eyebrows drew together. 'Thanks for the first two compliments, and cooking hasn't beaten me. I'm just not interested.'

He smiled. 'I must cook for you one night. I actually enjoy cooking.'

'I'll take you up on that when I run out of fast food.' She forced herself to try and at least look as calm as he was. But her nerves were jumping all over the place.

On the front of his shirt half a dozen dark hairs from his chest curled over the edge of the seam. She had trouble tearing her eyes off them. Heavens, it was hot in here.

He looked around. 'It looks different inside. A woman's touch, I suppose. I like the rug.'

'Thank you. I brought a few of my things but I've never owned much before. My idea of furnishing wasn't really appreciated in my mother's house. Too unsophisticated and homey.' She shrugged and smiled. 'As always, I'm free to do as I please here.'

'Do you remember kissing me fifteen years ago?'

She flinched against the cushions. Where had that come from? Startled, she looked across at his face. He was staring at her mouth and she consciously prevented herself from running her tongue across suddenly dry lips.

Savannah turned away and spoke to the rug they'd just discussed. 'I remember the occasion, yes. I thought you'd forgotten. You never spoke to me again after that.'

'Your uncle tanned my hide when he found out.'

That shocked her. 'He never said!'

'I didn't hold it against him. He said this was your place to be a child and he didn't want you to have to be a woman yet.'

'He told me you stayed away because you had no taste.'

Theo threw back his head and laughed. 'Cunning old devil. I really liked him. It's strange to be in his house, with him not around.'

'Yes, it is. So, why *are* you here, Theo?' She unconsciously placed her hand to her throat. She could feel the vibration between them. She felt like asking him how long he was staying, because she didn't think she could hold her breath much longer.

It was as if she'd suddenly become sensitised to everything about him and what it was doing to everything in her. If she was honest, it had been building up all week between them.

When he turned it on, she was powerless. She didn't even think he knew he was turning it on. It wasn't fair, it wasn't sensible...but it was exciting. She should get him out of here.

Theo looked at her from under half-closed lids. 'I'm not sure,' he replied. 'Call it a sudden impulse.'

He watched the pink flush in her cheeks and the

quickened rise and fall of her breasts under the ripe-plum-coloured gown. That was what she reminded him of. A small, round, yet firm, luscious plum. He could feel his pulse jump as the connotations set in. Even her eyes were plum purple in this light. She'd been on his mind since that hurt look he'd seen when he'd mentioned her mothering skills.

'I'll put the coffee-jug on.' Her voice seemed to come from a long way away yet he savoured every syllable. She got under his skin like an allergic re-action. Heating and burning and stinging him with desire. Just the sound of her incredibly sexy little voice was enough to make him want to see if she tasted as good as she looked.

He watched her stand, blink and then move jerkily to pass his chair on the way to the kitchen. His arm shot out of its own volition and caught her wrist. They both looked surprised at the sight of her small arm circled by his strong fingers.

'What are you doing?' she whispered, half-mesmerised.

'I don't know—but it sure as hell feels good.' He pulled her slowly backward towards him until she was off balance and leaned over him. Then he lifted his other hand and gently tipped her into his lap. She turned her face towards him. Her eyes were wide and her mouth looked soft.

Savannah's heart was pounding. Up close, Theo looked even better. But she would have been cooler sitting on the pot-bellied stove. She could feel all her strength draining away with the heat, and the tiny voice inside her head screaming for reason was barely a whisper.

When his mouth stopped a millimetre from hers, she sighed against him and they touched. She felt that first contact down to her toes. He feather-brushed her lips with his and she thought she would die from the tenderness. An ache grew inside her, demanding more, and her fingers crept behind his powerful neck to curl in his hair and pull his mouth against hers.

She heard him groan and his lips slid like silk on hers. Then his tongue touched just inside her lip and ran along the softness within. She moaned and parted her lips more as he deepened the kiss. Suddenly everything became centred on the sensual duel between two hungers.

She couldn't tell where the kiss started or finished, or how long it lasted. He filled her senses and drugged them until she knew she never wanted it to end. Finally, he drew away in tiny nibbles and slowly she surfaced.

Savannah opened her eyes. She was sprawled across him, her dressing-gown open and the swell of her breasts almost spilling from the lace V on the bodice of her nightdress.

He was watching her, and the hunger in his eyes belied his next comment.

'This may not have been a good idea. You do taste as good as you look. I think I'd better go.'

She wriggled to an upright position and then stood up. She shook her head, looked down on him in her uncle's chair and marvelled at her own response to a virtual stranger's kiss. It wasn't as if she'd never been kissed, for heaven's sake!

Theo had kissed her when she was fourteen but nothing like this! And she'd *lived* with Greg—but even that hadn't been anything like this. She put a hand to her head. She was repeating herself.

Theo met her eyes yet offered nothing further. Which left it up to her. She stifled a slightly hysterical giggle.

His technique had certainly improved! She barely restrained herself from touching her fingers to her lips in awe.

'I don't believe that happened.' She started to walk away but only succeeded in turning a circle. His eyes were very dark blue and she could almost feel his touch from the way he looked at her. 'Help!' she babbled nervously. 'You should be stamped "dangerous goods" or "flammable liquid" or something.'

'Savannah.' He caught her hand and she thought he was going to pull her down onto his lap again. Her heart pounded and she ran her tongue along dry lips.

'Hell, I wasn't going to do this,' he said, and did pull her down and fasten his lips to hers. This time they were even hungrier, and wherever his hands touched she wanted them to stay.

He pulled his mouth away and she turned her head, searching for his lips until she felt them on her neck. The exquisite sensations made the breath catch in her throat.

He came back to her mouth for a final tender salute and then stood up, pushing her in front of him. She swayed on her feet and he steadied her with his arm around her shoulders

She stepped away. 'Yes, I think you'd better go.' Her voice cracked. He smiled an odd, twisted smile and opened the door. Benson barked once and then the door shut behind Theo with a click.

She stood where he'd left her, listening to his fading footsteps on the verandah, and trembled. The sound of his car as it accelerated down her driveway made her wince.

When she'd been fourteen, she'd thought she would never forget her first kiss. Tonight's second and third from this man were going to be *much* harder to forget.

CHAPTER FIVE

THEO decided to ignore his impulses in future. Further visits to Savannah's house would be just too dangerous.

The next time he got involved with a woman he was going to stay in control and not be blinded by lust.

He only had one more day at work before his three days off and Theo tried to avoid Savannah as much as he could on Thursday morning. But it was hard— she seemed to be everywhere he turned.

Even the tea-lady sang Savannah's praises for getting someone to fix the squeaky wheel on her tea-trolley, which had been annoying her for months.

Julia peppered her conversation with 'Savannah said this' or 'Savannah says something else', and it grated on his nerves.

Nobody seemed to mind that she bulldozed them into doing things they normally wouldn't have tackled. Probably because she was in there, working harder than any of them. And always with a smile. He shook his head. He wasn't going to fall into that trap.

'Sister Laine?' His voice cut across the babble in the office during a quiet period. All conversations stopped. Savannah's head came up from the roster book she was working on.

Her eyes narrowed at his tone. 'Yes, Dr McWilliam?'

'There was a heavily pregnant woman in the waiting room ten minutes ago. Why haven't I seen her yet? Surely triage would have moved her towards the front of the line?'

'Because I sent her straight over to Obstetrics. All pregnant women over twenty-four weeks should be seen by the obstetric officer on call in the maternity unit and under the practised care of midwives, not outpatient staff.'

'Since when?'

'The circular was passed by Dr Ross this morning and should be in your pigeon-hole this afternoon.'

Theo had suggested such a practice several months ago but no one had actually done the paperwork. 'Why wasn't I told personally?'

She answered easily enough. 'Sorry about that. I was relying on all the outpatient doctors reading their pigeon-hole mail.' Savannah's face remained expressionless but there was something dancing in the back of her eyes. 'Of course, if we'd had a director of Emergency, I would have discussed it with him first.'

The sound of an approaching ambulance prevented Theo from commenting on her smart remark.

In the next five minutes the ward started to fill and they all slipped back into emergency mode.

A curly-headed man had blood dripping from one of his hands, despite the large towel wrapped around it.

'Looks arterial. I'll take this one.' Theo and Julia

ushered the man, who had been wood-working at home, into one of the minor surgery theatres.

A grubby youth in his late teens stumbled in, holding his jaw. Savannah could smell the alcohol from where she stood, and frowned.

'Can I help you?'

'Me bleedin' tooth is killin' me. It's been there for three weeks and I've had enough. I need the doctor.'

Savannah handed him a clipboard with an admission sheet to fill out. 'Doctor is with someone at the moment. If you sit here I'll ask him to see you as soon as he's free.'

An old farm ute pulled up beside the emergency entry.

Savannah excused herself and moved to help the elderly farmer's wife from the passenger seat. Her lips were blue-tinged and she clutched her chest. Savannah turned to the young toothache man. 'Grab that wheelchair, please, and slip it under this lady if you could.'

He looked at her sullenly for a moment before doing as he'd been bade. He gave the older lady a sour look. 'I suppose she gets to see the doctor before me now?'

Savannah narrowed her eyes and bit back the scathing life-or-death comment that came to mind. 'I'm afraid so. Perhaps you'd like to try one of the dental surgeries. If it is only the tooth, the doctor will have to refer you anyway.'

'I know me rights. I'll see the doctor.'

Savannah nodded, unsurprised. The incidence of people who 'knew their rights' was endemic in the city. There had to be some folk like that in the country, too. They were consumer-orientated and demanded attention, despite the necessity of triage in a hospital. Any seriously ill patient would naturally receive precedence over those less critical.

Savannah concentrated on her new patient and quickly wheeled the woman towards a bed. It was harder than Savannah expected to assist her to lie down.

'I need to raise the head of the bed, Mrs Jones. Have you done something to your back as well?'

'It's the lamingtonectomy, I had me back op'rated on four weeks ago,' she wheezed. 'Can't sit—just stand or lie flat.'

Savannah blotted out the sudden picture of a coconut-covered chocolate cake with an inner smile.

Laminectomy—without the 'ington'—was the surgical cutting of bone in the spine to give access to the spinal cord.

'That must be hard when you've difficulty breathing. I'll tilt the whole bed up by lowering your feet as well—that will keep your spine straight. This mask will give you some oxygen.'

Savannah reached across and positioned the green plastic mask gently over her patient's nose and mouth before connecting the woman to the monitors. 'I know that's uncomfortable, but it should help you to breathe easier.'

She pointed to the handful of wires she was sorting. 'These leads stick on your chest and tell us what your heart thinks of all this excitement.'

'The pain's in me side and it hurts to breathe in,'

Mrs Jones gasped. 'I was tryin' to finish makin' the pickles, then I coughed up some blood and it fair put the wind up me. The old man said to get up here pronto.'

'Your husband was right.' Mrs Jones closed her eyes and Savannah could see she was exhausted. 'Have you had any soreness in your leg?'

'Me left one was fair paining me this morning. It's been a bother for a couple of days now. Why?'

Savannah ran her hand over the hot and reddened area of Mrs Jones's calf. She shook her head in awe at the woman who'd continued her chores with a deep vein thrombosis and now a probable pulmonary embolism.

The blood clot Savannah suspected had lodged in her lung had probably originated from the clot in her leg. Thankfully it must be a smallish one but more could break off at any time.

'You're lucky you didn't keel over at the sink. Rest for a few minutes while I arrange for an X-ray of your chest and tell the doctor you're here.' In Sydney there would have been all sorts of sophisticated tests to prove the diagnosis. Theo would have to manage with a plain X-ray and some basic blood tests.

Savannah moved quickly from the cubicle towards the minor theatre, and was just in time to see Julia lift the last bandage from the curly-headed man's hand and step back.

The tiny artery sprang into life, pointed its severed end to the ceiling like a coiled snake and squirted a stream of bright blood high into the air. Theo swooped with the tiny forceps and caught it by the end, clamped it and then tied it swiftly off with a suture.

Savannah wasn't surprised his aim had been unerring. He could have been very successful in any branch of medicine. Such a waste.

'Got you, you little devil.' Theo glared at the offending vessel.

Savannah tried to bite her smile back, unsuccessfully. 'Looks like it got you, too,' she pointed out. A bright arc of blood had left a spectacular trail across Theo's chest. 'There's a new coat behind the door.' Her smile disappeared. 'Then I need you in cubicle five for a probable pulmonary embolism I'd like you to see before I risk moving her to X-Ray.'

He looked up at her over the top of his protective eyeglasses. 'Vital signs?'

'She's moderately hypertensive and her oxygen saturation is less than eighty-five per cent prior to oxygen. But I'm not happy with her. Looks like a DVT in her left leg, too.'

He turned back to the repair work on the man's hand. 'I'll be less than two minutes. The wound's not big…' he grinned at the gentleman who had his head turned away from the action on his own arm '…but Jack's drill slipped and it's deep.'

Savannah nodded and spun around to head back to her patient. The sound of an approaching siren made her sigh. Another half-hour between patients would have been nice. But that was the nature of the game in Emergency.

She directed the ambulance officers into another

cubicle with their trolley. A young woman lolled, semi-conscious, on the pillows.

'Overdose on Serepax.' The paramedic shook his head. 'Her boyfriend found the empty tablet packet beside her. He thinks it's less than two hours ago.'

'Right, I'll arrange some charcoal and sorbitol before she absorbs any more. We'll keep an eye on her respirations and consciousness level and then send her up to Intensive Care. They'll give her another dose of charcoal up there.' Savannah connected the woman's leads to her own machine to check heart rate and rhythm before waving to farewell the AOs.

'Try and give us half an hour before you come back with anyone else, please.' She crossed her fingers cheekily and they grinned back as they reversed their trolley out of the room.

She dashed to the office and quickly dialled the nursing supervisor's number.

'Hi, it's Savannah in Emergency. Can I have a spare registered nurse for half an hour, please? We're snowed under here and I need someone to keep a close eye on a critical patient.' She listened and nodded. 'That's great, thanks.'

She dropped the phone back into its cradle and turned to go back to the observation room.

'When will the doctor see me?' The toothache man had followed her into the office.

Savannah sighed. 'Please, return to the waiting room. The waiting time before the doctor sees you has increased so it will be at least another half-hour or longer if someone ill comes in.'

'No one else is gettin' in front of me.'

'I'm sorry, sir. This isn't a line in the supermarket. This is a hospital. A three-week-old toothache is seen to *after* critical patients. Now, please, return to the waiting room or I'll have to ask you to leave.'

He sneered in her face and his breath was heavily saturated in alcohol. 'You and whose army?'

'*My* army.' Theo gently put Savannah aside and stepped into the man's personal space.

The doctor towered over him and Savannah couldn't help smiling at the sudden change in the young man's expression. He seemed to shrink in front of her eyes.

Theo was spelling it out. 'If I catch you anywhere but the waiting room before you're called, I'll have you removed—or do it myself. Do you understand?' Theo's cold eyes bored into the smaller man's and he shuffled away and returned to his seat.

'Thanks.' She shrugged off the incident and picked up Mrs Jones's notes. 'She's in here and I've a woman with Serepax overdose in cubicle four when you're finished. Julia can start in there when she's free.'

Theo followed her. How could she be so calm when that guy had been trying to bully her? The creep could have turned very nasty. 'Right. I'll see her next.' He shook his head, then said, 'So that guy didn't worry you?'

'I've met jerks before. He's just the first since I started here.' She smiled at the elderly lady as they approached her bed. 'Mrs Jones, this is Dr McWilliam.'

Theo filed that away and looked at the woman

Savannah was concerned about. His brows drew together and he shot a look at Savannah. 'Why isn't she sitting upright?'

'She had a laminectomy four weeks ago and has to keep her spine straight.'

Theo grimaced. 'I should have known you'd have a reason. Sorry.' His assessment was thorough but quick. 'Right, X-ray, heparin infusion, bed-rest, stockings, and admit her to Intensive Care until she's stable.'

Mrs Jones's eyes filled with tears. 'Then I have to stay in?'

Theo patted her hand. 'I'm afraid so, Mrs Jones. The pain in your chest is probably a piece of a clot from your leg that has lodged in one of the blood vessels in your lung. The area of lung that's affected has just lost the greater part of its blood supply and that's where your pain is coming from. If it had been a big clot you could have died from the shock. You were very sensible, coming in.'

'Yes, Doctor. Will you explain it all to my husband?'

'Sure. Now, your body will break down that clot but we need to make sure you don't make any more while it's doing that or dislodge the rest of the one in your leg. I'm afraid you're on strict bed-rest for at least a couple of days and you'll have to put up with some blood tests and X-rays. Sister will fix that now.'

The day continued at a frenetic pace and by the time Savannah came to call the toothache man to see Theo, he'd gone.

* * *

A week later, Theo was driving home just before sunset. He'd had a rotten day—had diagnosed an advanced lung cancer on a fifty-year-old woman, and his lawyer had phoned to ask if he'd considered the remarriage option of Sam's custody fight.

As he drove past Savannah's gate, she was there, sliding a dozen eggs into the mailbox to sell. She had her back to him, wearing a pair of cheek-hugging shorts and a man's shirt knotted at the waist. Theo's mouth went dry and his car nearly ran into the ditch.

He knew the last time he'd been to her house things had got out of hand but, after all, it was only polite to stop. He worked with the woman, for heaven's sake. He'd be able to keep his distance.

He pulled the Range Rover over beside her and leaned his elbow out the window. When she smiled, his day marginally improved.

'Hi! Getting into sales now?'

She nodded. 'I've more eggs than I can eat. You look tired.'

She'd noticed. It made him feel better. His next words seemed to slip out involuntarily. 'Do you want to come back and see my place for an hour? It'll be dark soon but we've time for a quick look. It's been years since you were there and there's been quite a bit of renovation done on it.'

This wasn't keeping his distance. He gritted his teeth at the thought, but it would be nice to have someone to talk to for a change after a hectic afternoon. It had *nothing* to do with his lawyer's suggestion.

He saw her glance at her house and shrug. The

fading light made her eyes that deep purple he could lose himself in.

'I don't suppose it matters if the house is open.' She picked up Benson and tucked him under her arm. 'But I'm bringing my guard dog, so don't try anything.'

'I wouldn't dream of it. Hop in.' Suddenly he felt like whistling. He leaned across and opened the door for her, and a drift of what smelt like crushed violets floated across to him.

His car was out of practice, carrying females, and he threw a coil of rope and his doctor's bag over the seat to make room for her feet. His vehicle wasn't the only one out of practice with females. Why had he started this?

'So how was the rest of the afternoon at work?' She turned towards him as he changed gear, and her eyes were soft and inviting. He looked away from her face to the gearstick. It was very close to her thigh where the firm brown skin of her upper leg disappeared under her shorts. She had great thighs. He crunched into second gear and that made him smile. Get your hormones under control here, Theo.

'Obviously it was amusing.' She was still talking about the two hours of his shift after she'd gone home. Most of it had passed in a blur since today's phone call from his lawyer. Another setback in what was becoming a black comedy of setbacks.

As for work, he'd done his job competently even if he'd been a little distant with everyone else. Suddenly he didn't want to talk about work, but he had a feeling it would figure in most of Savannah's conversations. That was another reason he didn't want to get involved with her. It was too risky to mix business with pleasure.

She was staring ahead down the winding dirt road when he looked at her next. It made it easier to keep on track. He played back what her question had been. Got it. His afternoon at work. 'Busy, but we coped. How was your afternoon?'

'I think Louise is nearly ready to have her litter. I've put a bale of straw in the pigpen. I'll check her again when you bring me home.'

'Ring me if you need me.'

He saw the almost imperceptible shake of her head and grimaced to himself. 'But I'm sure you won't.' In the short time he'd known her he'd realised she was fiercely independent.

Unless it had to do with the hospital. Then it was OK for him to help.

He frowned. He must talk to Dr Ross about those strategies she wanted implemented. He fully intended to support her, although he wasn't going to tell Savannah that just yet. He knew she thought he was irresponsible—which was a joke when all he wanted to be was responsible. For his son.

He glanced across at her and caught her yawning. He'd noticed in the last day or two that she was starting to look tired.

'Am I that boring?'

'Yep.'

She grinned at him and he realised how much he enjoyed her company and that rare and sudden smile she didn't use enough. She'd run herself into the ground with two full-time jobs going but he couldn't help her unless she asked him.

She was such a tiny thing. He could have lifted her over his head if he'd wanted. The thought of his hands around her waist brought other images to mind. He was getting fixated here. Snap out of it! he ordered himself silently.

Luckily it only took a couple of minutes to arrive at his own gate and he was glad to get there. By now he was having a hard time keeping his hand on the gearstick and off her leg.

Savannah sat forward a little to glance around. Her lips parted in pleasure at the white Queenslander-style house with its railed verandahs and the moon-gate at the bottom of the wide front staircase.

'Your family has always had the grandest house in the valley. It's beautiful, Theo. But I don't remember it being so big.'

He enjoyed her reaction. The work on the house had been therapy for his frustration as the court case had dragged late into the second year. He hadn't appreciated the house as a whole until now.

'I've been renovating and adding on for the last couple of years. Keeps me busy.'

She put Benson down on the ground and Theo cupped her elbow lightly to escort her up the steps. 'Come in. I'll make you a drink and we can sit on the verandah and watch night fall before I show you inside.'

Savannah felt his hand on her arm like a branding iron. He'd branded her fifteen years ago when she'd been fourteen. Now she was back in his field. That made her brave or foolish, and she had a fair idea which one.

'Sounds fine.' She glanced at her watch. She'd ask to leave before the hour was up. There was Louise and the piglets to think about. Yeah, right, she mocked herself.

Theo left her leaning on the rail, looking over the paddocks, until he returned with two glasses and an open bottle of white wine.

'Do you like Verdelho?'

'I like most wines.' She really enjoyed a soft dry red but she wasn't a connoisseur, far from it. 'Can I have ice cubes?'

His eyebrows shot up. 'In Verdelho?' Then he laughed. 'Why not?' he said, and disappeared back inside. He looked so different when he laughed. Even more attractive. She remembered Julia saying he had lost his sense of humour. Obviously, she, Savannah, amused him. She frowned and then shrugged. She could cope with that.

He came back and her glass clinked with ice. He raised his own. 'Cheers.'

'Cheers.' She took a sip and looked at him from under her lashes. 'What did you think about the changes I need in the department?'

'Good luck.'

She narrowed her eyes in annoyance. Then he tipped the glass up and sipped at his wine. She watched the movement of his strong throat as he swallowed. There was something incredibly sexy in that motion and she couldn't tear her eyes away.

He glanced up and caught her staring, and his voice

held a smile. 'I'm teasing you. I'll help. But I think you're a determined woman, Savannah. Just don't expect to be greeted by shouts of enthusiasm—country towns accept change slowly.'

'What about you, Theo? Can you accept change?'

His eyes darkened and although he didn't answer her, she felt they'd moved to another level of communication. A physical one. She fought to keep her mind on spoken conversation. There was safety in that.

This was her goal she was talking about. Her chance to make a difference to the city's perception—and her mother's perception. It was just as important to deliver quality contemporary care in a country hospital as in a city one. This was her gift to her uncle and the place that had given her so many wonderful memories. She was going to achieve that and this cynical man wasn't going to stop her. 'We are going to have the most efficient and effective country emergency department in Australia when I'm finished. Are you going to help me?'

He raised his glass and sipped again. 'What are you going to do about the fact we don't have the facilities the city has? We don't have access to the scans and the seven-day-a-week X-ray facilities and advanced pathology procedures. Or the staff. That's the killer. We don't have the specialist staff—not even registrars, let alone actual specialists.'

She shook her head. 'That doesn't matter. I'm talking about first-line emergency care. We compensate with hands-on skill and intuition. And guts and determination. I see it every day. Because there isn't a specialist to call up and ask, people improve their own skills. I've seen your diagnostics in action and your broad range of very competent skills, from orthopaedics to obstetrics to ophthalmology. I'll bet the specialists can't do that.'

'Thank you, Sister Laine.' He bowed and then held up his hands. 'You'll do fine and I said I'd help you when you need me to.' He stepped up close to her until their shoulders were touching.

She couldn't help her awareness of his body heat against her and her mouth went dry.

Theo rubbed his shoulder against hers. 'Now can we talk about something else?'

She sighed and stared at his long fingers against the wood of the verandah railing beside hers. She remembered them holding her. 'What do you want to talk about, Theo?'

'The weather? Your farm? Why you moved here? Anything but the hospital.' He rested his glass on the rail.

Savannah grimaced. 'OK. What's happened to you in the last fifteen years, Theo?' She watched the change in his face and he stepped away until there was a hand's breadth distance between them. Oops. She almost hated the cool air circulating between them.

'I grew up.' He looked back at her and smiled bitterly. 'Apparently I became harsh, a loner and refused to be tied down.' He drained his glass.

She took another sip of her own and didn't dispute his claim. Then she added, 'You also became a very good doctor.'

'Thanks.' The comment was dry. 'Come and see the rest of the house and then I'll run you back.'

Inside was a beautiful home, with high beaten tin ceilings, freshly painted, and stained-glass casement windows. Not even a smear of dirt marred their perfection and the polished wooden floors were spotless.

She glanced sideways at him. 'Do you spend all your days off scrubbing this place?'

'I'm naturally tidy but, no.' He shrugged. 'I have a ferocious cleaning lady who comes in several times a week. Her husband's out of work and they're renting a run-down farmhouse further up the valley.'

He gestured for her to precede him. 'This entry comes through the kitchen.' The kitchen was huge. A long granite bench ran the full length and an old-fashioned kitchen table stood in the middle, complete with drawers underneath. Savannah had never seen so many appliances or so much bench space in a kitchen. He really must cook. And it was immaculate. She shrugged. Each to their own.

They walked through the dining room and into the hall with its cedar picture rail and carved archway. To the left were the bedrooms and to the right was the verandah again.

'What's in here?' She moved to open one of the doors, and to her surprise he leaned forward and rested his hand on the knob to prevent her.

'That one's private.' He steered her away towards the next door, which was the bathroom. Her brow furrowed and she glanced back at the closed door. 'So what's in there? Bodies of curious women?' He just smiled. 'OK, Bluebeard, show me the ones I can see.'

'The bathroom.' He gestured. A perfectly restored claw-footed bath stood under the huge wooden-framed window which looked out onto the largest of the jacarandas outside. There were no curtains, but feathery indoor plants trailed off the window-sill.

'Now, that's lovely. One of the joys of country living includes no neighbours to see in,' Savannah commented with a cheeky smile.

'Bedroom.' The master bedroom was plainly furnished and precisely tidy. No pictures, photos, rugs, plants or paraphernalia. She raised her eyebrows at it but he shrugged and didn't offer any explanation.

'Well, I know you didn't invite me because you wanted to seduce me in your romantic boudoir.'

He curled his lip. 'Romance isn't a tangible thing. It's where a woman sees it. Usually in an expensive setting, from my experience.'

'It was a joke, Mr Grumpy.'

She rolled her eyes and turned away from the bedroom. 'You do sound very bitter, Theo.' She glanced up at him, so tall beside her. Something had changed his mood. 'Maybe you haven't found the right woman yet. One day you'll find her and get married and have children.'

'Getting married and having children will make everything all right, will it?' He laughed bitterly.

'I said, with the *right* woman.'

'What about you, little Savannah, with your clever mouth that should be used for other things? Could *you* be that woman?' His eyes held a hint of danger and he ran one finger down her arm. 'And if I need a wife? Are you interested?'

She couldn't suppress the shiver of awareness but that didn't mean he had it all his own way. She met his sardonic look with a measuring one of her own. 'Why do I get the impression you're trying to frighten me off?' He gave a short, harsh laugh and didn't deny it.

'I've already been a temporary wife.'

He raised his eyebrows as if to say, 'Tell me more.' But she shook her head.

'It's not much fun. Thanks for the flattering offer but for now I think you should take me home.'

Savannah walked back up the long hallway toward the safety of the verandah. Benson greeted her like a long-lost friend and she slid her hand under his furry stomach and picked him up. 'Let's go home, mate.'

They didn't speak on the short drive. When Theo pulled up at her front steps, he kept the engine running. The house was in darkness and his lights shone to her door.

'Thank you for an interesting evening.'

'My pleasure.' He saluted.

As soon as she'd turned the verandah light on, he reversed out and drove away. 'Well, it didn't look like a pleasure to me,' she said to the departing car.

She stroked the curls between the dog's ears. 'Well, that was an unusual hour, young Benson. I wonder what he meant by *if* he needed a wife?' She frowned and shook her head. 'Let's get a torch and check on Louise.'

Louise had done it without her. Or almost all of it.

There were two white piglets floundering about in the straw, searching for their mother, with their tiny eyes closed. Five more were anchored euphorically to their mother. Number eight arrived a minute after Savannah had propped the two against their mother's side. Luckily, Louise didn't seem to mind her mistress's intervention.

This one was smaller than the rest and wasn't moving. Savannah forced herself to give nature a chance without interference but after twenty seconds, which felt like twenty hours, she yanked her hanky from her pocket and wiped his tiny face. Still no movement. She rubbed the cloth up and down his tummy but the little body just flopped around with the movement.

'Come on, you. I have no desire to do mouth-to-mouth on a piglet.' Still no movement. She sighed and laid him belly up on her palm and loosely curled her other fist to make a tunnel to blow through. She puffed down the palm tunnel onto his mouth and nose and then tapped his chest a few times with one finger.

No movement.

She puffed again and tapped his chest with a pig's version of external cardiac massage. This time he shuddered under her fingers. She puffed again and stopped worrying about his heartbeat. He wouldn't be moving unless it was there.

Now he was squirming and she smiled as she placed him against his mother's teat. The tiny mouth wavered back and forth in front of the tantalising smell he was programmed to seek.

Savannah sat back on her heels and grinned like an idiot. Today definitely had had highs and lows.

Exhausted, but satisfied, she wished Theo had been there. She thought about this evening at his house. She had a feeling she was going to toss and turn for a while when she went to bed. Why would Theo need a wife?

On their days off over that weekend and during the next week, Savannah saw little of Theo except at work. He appeared even more distant than usual. Nothing was mentioned about his strange comment and she wondered if it had been a bizarre way of asking her to sleep with him.

Who could figure out men? She didn't need the hassle. She had enough to worry about.

It felt like Louise's litter had started a run of farm-related problems. Bruce the boar looked unwell and Savannah had to ask the vet to come and see him. He ordered a daily regime of antibiotic injections for the large boar that tried her skills and strength to the ut-most to administer.

She almost asked Theo for help but cautioned her-self not to rely on him or anyone. She'd trusted peo-ple before and had been let down. She could do this on her own.

Then a fox caused havoc and tragic destruction in the hen-house and she had to replace a whole section of wire around the fowl enclosure to stop a massacre.

When one of the cows, with calf at foot, came down with mastitis and refused to allow her calf to feed, Savannah had a milking chore and then bucket-feed of the neglected baby to add to her duties. It didn't help that the ward was constantly busy and she was getting off late more often than not.

Dark rings appeared around her eyes and her hands were work-roughened and painful from the constant stream of farm tasks which seemed never-ending after the long shifts.

'Let me give you a hand on the farm while it's so busy.' Theo stopped her one afternoon as she came off duty. 'I could do the pigs in the mornings before work and that would give you an extra hour to take it easy when you come home.'

'I'm not doing long shifts like you, Theo. I'll be all right.'

'I get a three-day weekend every week. I could do Friday's chores for you.'

She was tempted but she'd always had trouble accepting help from others. It seemed the times she'd trusted someone else had been some of the most painful of her life. It was better this way. 'No, thanks.'

Theo narrowed his eyes and stepped back. 'As you wish.'

Savannah avoided his eyes and then turned for home. Now she felt guilty. The guy should be pleased she didn't want to impose on him.

After the weekend she was exhausted and during the week was in bed almost before Theo finished work in the evenings.

The depressing feeling that it was all getting on top of her sapped her energy more.

It had nothing to do with the fact that Theo hadn't dropped around to see how she was coping.

*   *   *

On the Friday of the next week they finally had a quiet day with few emergencies. Savannah arranged another appointment with the medical superintendent and outlined her concerns regarding the personal pagers and the cannulation course.

He promised to look into it and she had to be content with that. She'd speak to him again.

Julia was downstairs in the cafeteria at lunch and Theo had gone to the medical ward to see a patient. The orderly who was normally around had been called away and Savannah was alone.

The outpatient bell rang and she walked down to answer it. It was the toothache youth from a few weeks previously. He looked unhealthily pale but innocuous enough. At least he didn't smell of alcohol this time. He had a bloodstained scarf tied around his grubby wrist and held his left hand gingerly in his right as if it was injured.

'Can I help you?' She watched his eyes flick past her and he shuffled his feet in his battered shoes.

'Cut myself. Have a look.' His words ran together and were hard to distinguish between his thin lips.

Savannah frowned and felt the first twinges of unease. 'Come through to the cubicle and I'll take off the bandage.' She gestured for him to precede her up the corridor and he moved reluctantly ahead of her.

His head swivelled as he went, as if looking for something, and the tension vibrated almost palpably from his body while his blond hair hung lank and straggly to his shoulders.

She glanced up the corridor herself, hoping someone else would enter the ward.

He sat on the bed in the cubicle and held out his wrist.

Stalling, Savannah slowly pulled on some disposable gloves and leaned reluctantly towards the injured limb.

Suddenly the scarf fell away and the hand below lifted and magically produced a knife. It was short and wicked-looking and she felt the breath freeze in her throat.

His other hand fastened around her wrist and twisted her arm up behind her back. The point jagged against her shoulder-blade through her uniform.

A tiny gasp passed her lips before she could drag herself back under some control. Steady, she warned herself. He's probably high as a kite and on the edge.

'I'll get served first today, sweety. Where's your drugs?'

Where was Theo?

CHAPTER SIX

SAVANNAH forced her head to clear.

The standard procedure for this was capitulation.
Don't be heroic and turn a hold-up into a murder.
They'd drummed it into the staff at her old hospital
to give the assailant whatever he wanted. The rest was
up to the police.

The thought had galled her but that had been the
protocol. Now on the receiving end of a situation, she
could see the reasoning. Whatever they wanted wasn't
worth a life.

'In the office through here.' Her voice wavered but
strengthened towards the end of the sentence.

She started to drag in a deep breath but the expan-
sion of her lungs made the knife bite into her skin.
She changed her mind. Shallow was good. Where was
Theo? Or anybody? She tamped down a sob.

They stood together slowly and moved in almost a
frogmarch to the office. She forced herself to notice
anything distinguishable about him for the police later
as they moved. It kept her mind off the knife that
could snuff out her life with one push.

They halted in the office. 'I have to get the keys
out of my pocket.'

'No tricks.' The knife dug in a little more and she
could smell his unwashed body and the scent of fear.
He had a skull earring in one ear, she told herself.

Her heart was thumping and she could feel the adrenaline start to pump around her body. Fight or flight. To hell with flight. It made her feel reckless with anger.

The little creep. She'd like to push a knife into his back and see how he liked it. Settle, she warned herself. Remember the protocol.

Theo and Julia couldn't believe what they were seeing in the circular mirror at the corner of the ward. The sight of the man threatening Savannah with a knife hit Theo in the gut like a sledgehammer. He quelled his first impulse and whispered to Julia, 'Tell Switchboard Code Black, Emergency Ward,' he whispered, and then ignored her. He strolled towards the office as if he hadn't seen what was going on.

'Stop there or she's dead.' The teenager's voice broke on the final word and Savannah winced as the thug leaned the knife harder against her.

Theo felt the point as if it were in contact with his own skin. He lifted his hands in a placatory gesture and ensured his voice was calm and reasonable. Inside he was raging. 'I've stopped. Tell me what you want, we'll give it to you and then you can leave.'

'Get me the drugs. She's got the keys. Get them off her and open the cupboard.'

Theo flinched as the assailant stretched the curve of Savannah's spine backwards even further and he knew he would never forget the small sound of distress she made. The rage inside him bubbled and frothed at the edges of his control but unplanned movement was just not on. It was too dangerous for Savannah. He gritted his teeth.

The police would be here soon and would catch the idiot as soon as he left. He needed to get this finished before Savannah was hurt or they ended up with a hostage situation. Theo didn't trust himself if the youth tried to take Savannah with him. 'Let's do it, then.' He looked at Savannah. 'Which pocket?'

'Left.' He barely heard the whisper and felt like grabbing her and shielding her with his own body. He poured as much reassurance into his eyes as he could. Lord, she was brave.

He reached forward slowly.

'No tricks, you mongrel.' The youth's voice cracked again.

'We just want you out of here, mate. The drugs aren't worth getting hurt for.'

He slid his hand into Savannah's warm pocket and lifted the chain of keys slowly into view. 'It will all be over in a minute, sweetheart,' Theo reassured her quietly. He stepped back, shook the keys at the assailant and moved slowly to the drug cupboard so as not to alarm him.

When the square door of the cupboard was open, Theo stepped back and held out his hand for Savannah.

'Let her go. Take what you want and leave.'

The teenager's eyes darted between Theo, the woman he was holding and the open door of the drug cupboard. He bit his lip.

This was the most dangerous moment.

Savannah hadn't thought she could be any more

terrified and she'd prayed for Theo to come. Now he was here she was petrified.

Petrified that something would happen to him.

She was more scared that he would tackle the thug and be killed himself than that anything would happen to her. She could feel the tension in the thin arms holding her and she willed the creep to push her at Theo and out of his way.

'Get me a bag to put it in.'

'Right.' Theo's voice was very deep as he gritted his teeth. He reached down, upended the wastepaper bin and pulled the plastic bag lining it into his hand. He stepped up to the cupboard, swept the two shelves of contents into the bag and held out his hand for Savannah.

The youth still wavered and Theo's eyes narrowed. His voice was arctic. 'Let her go. You don't want that problem.' He held up the bag. 'Take it and go.'

Savannah held her breath until suddenly she felt the knife leave her back and she was pushed away. She landed against Theo's chest and didn't see the young man leave as her nose was buried in Theo's shirt. His arms circled her and he crushed her tightly against him.

Reality receded for a moment, and she inhaled his scent.

'Savannah. Are you all right?' His voice rumbled in his chest against her face and she felt a small hiccup of hysterical laughter in her throat. She swallowed it back and nodded her head.

She drew as much of a steadying breath as she

could, held firmly against him, and her voice was faint when she tried to talk.

'If I don't suffocate in here.'

He hugged her fiercely once more then held her away from him by her arms. The look on his face as he stared down at her almost brought tears to her eyes. He was devastated.

'I should have beaten the hell out of that guy last time he was here. I'm taking you home.'

That fired her up. 'You couldn't have known. And I'm not going home. We'll both stay here and finish our shifts.'

His eyes narrowed but before he could speak she forestalled him. 'I couldn't face an argument.' She dashed a hand across her eyes. 'Actually, I can't face going home yet.'

His hold loosened and he pulled her against him again, gently this time. She rested her cheek against the softness of his shirt and that was how Julia and the others found them.

Theo looked up but didn't let her go. 'Did they get him?'

Julia's voice quivered. 'Yes, as soon as he left. Are you OK, Savannah?'

She stepped out of Theo's arms and back to reality. She sank wearily into an office chair. 'I think I need a cup of tea.' She gave Julia a slight smile, and her chin wobbled.

'How about medicinal brandy?'

Theo answered for her. 'Ten mils wouldn't go astray.' He looked up as a burly police officer entered the office just as an ambulance drew up.

He helped Savannah to her feet. 'Go down to the staffroom with the sergeant. Try and eat something. I'll be down in a minute if your precious ward lets me.'

For once Savannah was glad to be told what to do. She rose shakily to her feet and led the way back down the corridor. She could feel Theo's eyes on her the whole way. Somehow that made her feel more protected than the large policeman walking beside her.

By the time she had gone over it all again for the policeman, Theo still hadn't come. They must be busy. She felt sick and desperately needed to think of something other than the events of the morning. She went back to work.

Savannah felt as if she were on the other side of a pane of glass from the rest of the world. Voices seemed muted and her response to questions was two seconds later than it normally would be.

What would have happened if Theo hadn't been there with her? Theo seemed to be only a glance away for the rest of the shift. She felt safe but uncomfortably like she was under a microscope.

At four o'clock Theo was busy with a patient and she slipped away before he finished. Now she wanted to go home. Alone. She had a feeling he wouldn't be pleased with the idea.

Julia had offered to come home with her, but Savannah wanted some time to herself. She knew Theo would drop in after work and she needed to gain some equilibrium before then. Otherwise she was going to throw herself into his arms and demand he wrap himself around her.

Benson sensed something was wrong and didn't leave her side when she came home. He must have known that he helped by being there. With extreme heroism he even accompanied her down to the pens to watch over her while she fed the pigs.

She took him into the bathroom after that while she had her shower and he curled up on the bathroom floor and guarded the door. She couldn't believe the little dog was so understanding. But her nerves were still shot.

She was dismayed to feel herself jumping at every odd sound. She'd never been timid and the weakness she felt inside horrified her. Late in the afternoon, dressed in her nightgown and robe after her shower, she went around and secured the house. There was no one to see into her windows but she even pulled the blinds down, something she'd never felt the need to do before.

At six-thirty Benson barked even before the lights of Theo's car shone onto Savannah's face where she stood at the verandah window, waiting.

'I see him. Good boy.'

Savannah leant down and smoothed the dog's curls before stepping out onto the verandah.

Theo had worried about Savannah as soon as he'd found out she'd gone. She'd looked to be coping but he didn't believe she was that composed on the inside. But she'd shut him out as usual. If it hadn't been so busy he'd have left earlier, and by the time he arrived at her house his mood was less than sunny.

He wasn't even on the verandah before he started to speak. 'Why did you leave without me? I would have come home with you and gone back when you'd settled.'

She lifted her head. 'Hello, Theo.' Her voice was dry.

He stepped up to her and held her upper arms. 'You should have told me you were ready to leave. It's no sin to ask a friend for help.' He hadn't intended to hassle her but he could feel the wall she was putting up to hide behind. She didn't have to be alone.

She turned away but not before he could see the tears in her eyes. 'Don't.' Her voice broke.

He winced. He was an insensitive fool. 'Oh, hell.' He came up behind her and pulled her back to rest against him. 'I'm sorry.' He massaged her arms. 'I've been reliving the danger you were in today as I drove out here, and I could strangle that mongrel—but I've no right to take it out on you.'

He turned her gently towards him until her nose rested against his shirt. 'I was terrified for you today, Savannah.'

She sighed against him. His chest was warm and comforting and she felt as if nothing could hurt her. Except him. She didn't want to move but she did.

She stepped away. 'I've rehashed it enough—could we, please, not talk about it any more?'

Theo turned his back on her and stared out over her paddocks. 'I saw Dr Ross. The pagers for all the nurses will arrive next week.' He turned back to face her and the lines of his face were self-derisive. 'Too late but done now. I'm sorry, Savannah. I should have acted sooner.'

She ran her finger down his cheek. 'You couldn't have known. Do you want to come in?'

He met her eyes. 'I want to come in.' He caught her hand and his voice dropped. 'And if you want me to, I'd like to stay tonight.' He gave her a crooked smile. 'I'll sleep on the lounge—just in case you wake up and you're worried.'

Savannah felt the breath catch in her throat. She'd been dreading the night.

Did she want him to stay because she was afraid to be alone or because it was what she'd wanted long before the danger of today? She stepped away from him and opened the screen door into the house. 'I'll be fine. You don't have to stay.'

She had a feeling he knew how she felt.

He showed her his open palms. 'I'm not doing it for you. It's my nerves that I can't settle.' He caught her arm, holding it until she turned to face him again. 'Will you protect me, Savannah?' His smile was tilted and she couldn't help smiling back.

'A big strong man like you? Now, why do I find that hard to believe?' She shook his arm off gently. 'All right, you can stay. But I'm not cooking for you.'

'I picked up frozen pizza.'

'Goody. That's Benson's and my favourite tea.'

After the meal, they cleared up together and then went to relax in the lounge room. Savannah perched uneasily on her chair but what she wanted to do was curl up in Theo's lap with his arms around her. She looked up and his eyes were on her.

'Come here.' He rose from the padded chair and leaned towards her to help her up. When he took her fingers, the warmth from his seeped into her. Her hand lay passively in his as she let herself be drawn into his embrace. When he wrapped himself around her, the tension dropped from her shoulders. It was bliss.

He took a couple of steps backward and pulled them both down into his chair, and she curled in a ball on his lap with her head on his chest.

Tears stung her eyes but it wasn't because of today. It was as if something she'd always searched for had appeared in the most unexpected place. It was the feeling of finding the warmth of arms around her that she'd never had.

Greg had never had it and she realised now how lucky she was that his real wife had turned up, wanting him back.

Of course Theo was only offering sympathy and comfort and she wept for the dream of someone in her life who would be there for her no matter what.

She felt his hand stroke her hair.

'Are you OK?' His voice was a rumble under her cheek and she wiped the dampness from her face as she strove for composure.

'Yes. I'm being very demanding here, but just hold me.'

'Demand away.' She could hear the smile in his voice. 'I'm feeling very safe from the bogeymen myself.'

'So that's why you said you needed a wife?' She felt him stiffen beneath her and wished the words unsaid.

'Forget I said that. How about we just have an affair? Much more fun.' He grinned lewdly at her.

She gave a half-laugh and shifted her body so she could look into his face. That was a mistake.

He bent his head and captured her lips with the sweetest kiss. She felt like she'd come home. Then the sweetness changed to passion as Theo leaned more firmly into her. It took on a vibrant urgency as if the sudden memory of today highlighted the precarious hold they both had on their destinies.

He lifted her to face him more directly and demanded a response that she couldn't deny. He groaned and she exulted in the knowledge she had the power to stir this man.

When she clutched his hair, he slipped his hand inside the neckline of her dressing-gown to cup her breast through the satin on her nightdress. Her kiss deepened and his hand tightened. His fingers slid the slippery material back and forth against her hardened nipple as the heat continued to build between them.

'Take me to bed, Theo. I need to feel all of you.'

She felt his sudden stillness. Then he asked, 'Are you sure?'

She met his eyes and nodded.

He moved with impressive strength to stand with her in his arms and carry her into her room.

He smiled slightly at the frilly cover on the double bed and sat her gently on the side. He pulled the sash on her dressing-gown free and slid the gown from her shoulders.

She sat there, strangely paralysed as his gaze slid over her body clad in the satin nightdress.

His beautiful eyes smouldered with passion at the sight of her and his voice was a whisper. 'Lovely nightgown, Savannah.' He grinned. 'But it has to go so I can feel your skin against mine.' And he captured her wrists in one hand to raise her and drew the satin over her head with the other. She stood before him clad only in the tiny scrap of her lace bikini pants and then she slid them off.

He reached past her and flipped back the frilly quilt before lifting her again. The roughness of his shirt scraped against her sensitised skin and she closed her eyes. He made her feel like a precious piece of porcelain as he lowered her carefully into the middle of the bed. It seemed as if she had closed her eyes only for a second before she felt his naked body slide against hers until they lay fused together like a face against a mirror.

'Your skin feels like velvet,' he said, then the rest was discussed with his lips and tongue and gently demanding hands as he worshipped her body as no one else ever had.

His hands and mouth were sometimes firm and erotic, sometimes so gentle she barely felt his touch, and always increasing the spiralling tension within her until she writhed beneath his hands and he beneath hers.

She grabbed at his head to pull his mouth back to her lips and she brushed the tips of her breasts across the iron of his chest. She felt reborn and exultant, powerful yet a captive of the turbulent storm they tossed in together.

He rolled away for a moment and she heard the rustle of protection, and she smiled. That made both of them careful. He rolled onto his back and his large hands cupped her buttocks with a sureness of intent. She found herself manoeuvred above him to sit astride his legs, and his hands moved to weigh each ripe breast as they swayed in offering above him.

Then he lowered her onto him.

Afterwards, she lay with her head on his chest, stunned that what had passed between them had been an earthly experience. And she'd thought he should be labelled dangerous after only a kiss!

'You OK?' The smile in his voice brought one to her lips.

'I think you just took me for a ride.'

'What?' He raised his eyebrows, not sure he liked the analogy.

'A beautiful, star-laden ride in a chariot of fire.' She kissed the springy dark curls and the solid wall of chest beneath. 'Now, shh.'

He closed his eyes again and she lay there until the deeper rise and fall below her cheek signalled he was asleep.

Gently she lifted his arm and moved to the edge of the bed. She drew the quilt over his sleeping body and leaned towards him to look down at him. She'd known he'd be sinfully erotic but not how generous he would be. Theo had given her a beautiful gift but such was his power she needed time to think.

She pulled her robe over her nakedness and belted it loosely, before padding out to the verandah to lean on the rail.

The stars were out in their millions and the five stars of the Southern Cross seemed closer than ever. Benson came to stand beside her, but it was as if he sensed she didn't need him to protect her any more, and he went back to his basket.

No, she didn't need him. She didn't need anyone. Somehow Theo had restored her balance and sense of self. For that she would always be grateful.

But there was a real risk of losing herself in this man. Did she want that with someone who was averse to commitment? What if she trusted him to always be there for her? What then if he tired of her? She realised she was over her hurt from Greg, but with Theo she didn't think she would recover so easily.

CHAPTER SEVEN

WHEN Theo woke to find Savannah gone, he sighed, unsurprised. She was as elusive as the wind. Their time together had been as incredible as he had feared it would be. Just thinking of her body, both firm and round, a delight and so receptive to his touch, stirred his desire. But what then?

He'd thought he held the monopoly on not getting involved but Savannah had a way of shutting doors that he could only admire.

He threw the quilt back and put his feet to the floor. Where was she?

He found her on the verandah. 'So, what are you thinking about?' he asked.

She'd heard the door open but didn't turn to look at him until she heard his voice.

'The stars are beautiful.'

'So are you.' He leant on the rail beside her. 'Aren't you going to tell me, then?'

She looked away again. 'Tell you what?'

'What you're thinking about.'

'I'm thinking I'll be all right now if you want to go home.'

He leant across and tucked his finger under her chin to turn her face towards him. 'Is that what you want?'

'I think so, yes.'

He gave a short laugh. 'OK. Can I get dressed first?'

He was taking it very well—but maybe he was glad to escape. She supposed it might have sounded a bit harsh but she was fighting for self-preservation.

'What are you afraid of, Savannah?'

'I'm sorry, Theo. As much as I'm sure it would be lovely to wake up with you beside me tomorrow morning, I don't want to get used to it.'

'Getting used to it frightens you?'

'Let's just leave it. Thank you for the pizzas.' For a moment she thought he was going to say something hurtful about what else he should be thanked for, but he just raised one eyebrow and dropped a kiss on her cheek, before turning to go inside.

Now she felt in the wrong again. How did he do that?

Some time during the night, Savannah woke and missed Theo beside her. By morning, Savannah couldn't help the erotic fantasy of how different things would have been if Theo were still there. Better not to get used to it.

Actually, she was feeling particularly feminine this morning.

She felt wonderful.

Savannah spun around and grinned to herself as she chose her laciest underwear. Theo had certainly saved her from wondering what the commotion about sex had been.

Now she knew.

Compared to yesterday's crushed-victim syndrome

and appalling loss of confidence, she now felt she could tackle the world. In fact, the more she thought about it, the more she wondered whether she'd over-reacted in asking him to go last night.

As long as she realised he wasn't responsible for dealing with her insecurities, why not consider that affair he'd mentioned? She'd have to think about that one.

Fridays were Theo's days off and Savannah couldn't help feeling relieved she didn't have to face him at work until she could be sure just what she wanted and didn't want. But she did seem to have a zing in her step, just thinking about it.

When she bounced into work, Julia couldn't hide her surprise at Savannah's resilience.

'I have to admit, Savannah, I can't believe you came in after yesterday. I reckon I'd take to my bed for a month after that horrible experience.'

'You should have seen me last night. I was a gibbering wreck.'

'So what happened?'

'I guess I decided that life is a risk and can be taken away when you least expect it. I'd better darned well enjoy it.'

What really surprised her was that people she'd had only the briefest acquaintance with since she'd started at the hospital came into Emergency to check she was OK after the previous day's ordeal.

It was heart-warming that they considered her enough of one of them to make the effort. Most offered their condolences on the loss of her uncle as well, and a few even remembered her from previous visits to the area as a child.

By the end of the day she felt as if she did have other friends and was a welcome member of the community. Bendbrook, her sleepy country town, was opening its arms to Savannah Laine, and it felt wonderful.

The highlight of the day was Dr Ross's visit. Theo had been to see him and this was official agreement to her cannulation course, pagers and computers. She deputised Julia to help her with the groundwork to get it all up and running.

By the time she was ready to go home she was tired, coming down from the euphoria of the morning, but she felt she could now face Theo with composure.

Until she saw the note on her kitchen table.

Dear Miss Independence
Try and accept this in the spirit it is offered. I've done your chores and invite you to a home-cooked meal at the McWilliam residence. I will call for you and your guard dog at 6 p.m. Theo.

She had to laugh. Cheeky blighter. She'd said she didn't want any help but just this once it was nice not to be responsible for the animals.

By six she was ready and the butterflies in her stomach were surely due to hunger rather than nerves. After four changes of clothes, she had settled for a long maroon skirt and white knitted cotton top. She tugged at the neckline, worried that it dipped too low into her cleavage, but the sound of Theo's car coming up the driveway signalled that her time had expired.

At least her hair bounced with a life of its own and she shrugged as she grabbed her matching white cardigan. It would do.

Theo laughed out loud at Benson, attired in a maroon bow around his neck. 'That's to let me know you two are a pair, is it?'

She waved a bottle of vintage port at him. 'I don't keep fancy wines, so I hope you like port after dinner.'

'I love port. In fact, I'm partial to anything that comes in plum colours. You look especially lovely tonight, Savannah.'

'Thank you for the compliment, sir, and also for your kind invitation. *And* for taking over the animals today.'

He raised one eyebrow sardonically. 'I'll bet that was hard to say.'

'Yes, it was.' She shrugged. 'But, then, my manners are better than yours.'

'You're right.' He grinned wickedly and opened the car door for her. 'Thank you for coming, Savannah.'

'Said the spider to the fly,' she said as she settled into her seat.

He smiled and shut the door.

As she waited for him to come around to his side of the car she acknowledged it was this feeling of exhilaration that she'd missed before she'd met Theo. It was fun, battling wits and trying to stay one step ahead of him. They both had baggage and maybe it was a race to see who dropped theirs first.

The drive was over swiftly and it promised to be a glorious sunset over the distant hills later. The house looked even more lovely at this time of the day and the jacarandas along the driveway were magnificently purple.

Theo had set up a small table and chairs on the verandah with nibbles and a bottle of white wine in an ice bucket.

'You were pretty sure I'd come tonight, weren't you?'

'Ah, but your manners are better than mine are, remember. It wouldn't have been polite not to come.'

She acknowledged that with a wry smile and, instead of sitting down, leant on the rail. 'I could look at this view for ever. I've forgotten the name of that mountain.'

'Banda Banda. It's pretty rugged and steep and they've lost the odd plane in one of the secret valleys that hide there.'

'You sound like you know it well.' She turned to look at him and the sun dug auburn highlights out of his dark brown hair. He looked very much the wealthy man on the land, with his well-cut jeans and his checked shirt open at the throat. She remembered the feel of his throat against her fingers, strong and firm, and that hollow where it joined his upper body that she'd dipped her fingers into before running them down his wonderful chest.

'Hello, Savannah?' His expression was quizzical. 'Fading out, woman?'

She blinked and realised he'd been speaking to her. Talk about sex-crazed! She felt the heat in her cheeks and lowered her head so he couldn't see her expression. 'Sorry, I lost the plot for a minute there.'

'Hmm.' He turned to the table and asked, 'Would you like a glass of Semillion now or a sherry?'

'Sherry, actually. There's something decadent about drinking sherry at sunset.'

'Let's be decadent by all means.' She could hear the undercurrents in his voice as he filled two of the smaller glasses, and realised she wasn't the only one who was thinking of last night.

To hell with it. This was life. She was going to enjoy it.

Theo didn't know what had brought about the change but that sudden smile he loved was on tap. He felt more blinded by that than by the red ball of fire setting over the far mountains.

It had been a gamble, setting all this up, but it had been worth it. He hadn't known how she would take his interference on the farm.

She'd been looking so tired lately, but he knew he would have to be careful not to alienate her with too many offers of help.

It was her turn to recall him to the conversation. 'I was asking about your knowledge of Banda Banda.'

He looked across at the huge bluff in the distance. 'I spent a couple of days up there with a rescue team, and it was pretty hairy. The plane we were searching for wasn't found until twenty-four hours later and the occupants were in a bad way by the time we got there.'

'How'd you get involved with that?'

He grinned. 'Your uncle volunteered me. I'd only been back on the farm for a couple of weeks and was fairly morose after a painful divorce and not working at the hospital. When the accident happened, your uncle rode around on Billy and told me to get off my butt and help out.' His lips tilted. 'So I did. After that we met up at least once a week for a chat and he nagged me into starting work at the hospital ''until something else comes up'' and, of course, I'm still there.'

'So why don't you make it permanent and take on the Director of Emergency job?'

'Don't you start.' He stiffened and turned away. 'I have my reasons, one of which is my inability to do justice to that position—at the present time.'

She stared at his handsome profile, highlighted by the last of the sun's rays. She'd known he'd been married, and divorced. Perhaps that explained a few things. 'And the other reasons are…?'

'Not something I want to talk about.'

'Ouch!' She grimaced but touched his arm. 'That's right up there with me sending you home last night.'

He gave one of his bitter laughs but his shoulders relaxed. 'And on that note I'd better check our dinner.' He squeezed her fingers resting on his arm as if to reiterate his desire for no further comment on that subject. 'Let me pour you a glass of wine before I disappear and do my Cinderella-in-the-kitchen bit.'

'I'll pour wine for both of us if I can follow you in and watch Cinders in action.'

'Bring the bottle, then.'

She watched him stride across the wooden boards of the verandah and couldn't help a last jolt of curiosity about his attitude to tying himself down at the hospital. She sighed and moved to collect the wine and glasses.

When she entered the kitchen her eyes widened. 'Impressive. It's like an operating theatre.'

Small dishes were set in lines, each holding what she guessed were strictly measured amounts of ingredients. Some were partially cooked and covered with cling wrap and a large bowl of steaming fried rice stood on the bench. An open cookbook was propped in a splatter-proof cookbook-holder and two chrome woks held pride of place on the big stove.

He glanced up as she stared at the table. 'Hope you like Chinese. We're having a banquet.'

'Love it.' She giggled. 'Benson and I love all types of take-away.'

'This is home-cooked take-away—my favourite—so you'd better love it more. First course is nearly ready. The table's in the dining room. Can you move the wine in there?'

She gazed in awe as he spread crushed prawns onto slices of bread and topped them with sesame seeds. 'Um, OK.'

She admired the bowls, chopsticks and Chinese spoons set for two. A squat candle sat in the middle of the table next to a small pile of paper napkins. She was still nonplussed at his ability to prepare a Chinese banquet. She'd have been a psychological mess if she'd ever been mad enough to try it. So he could do the cooking.

All thought processes stopped as she clarified that thought.

She'd meant, when she came to his house he could cook. It was unsettling to imagine them being in a steady relationship where chores were designated. But she already had him doing all the cooking!

'Sesame prawn toast, madam?' He placed the fried rice, a tray of golden brown triangles of toast and a large bowl of short soup in the middle of the table, then sat down.

'This is incredible. Where did you learn to do this? And why?'

Theo put down the ladle he'd been using to fill their bowls and sat back. 'That sounds sexist to me. Now, if I were a woman who liked to cook, would you be as surprised? I enjoy it. I don't do it often but I like to go the whole hog when I do.'

She didn't have a complex about her inability to master cooking. 'I'm not complaining. It looks fabulous and I'm starving.'

'Good. It's never as nice reheated the next day.'

That course was followed by sweet and sour pork, Mongolian lamb and satay chicken. Savannah put down her fork—she'd given up on chopsticks—and sighed. 'Stop. Don't put anything else on my plate. I can't eat any more. I'm as full as a toad and we've hardly touched the wine.'

'Well, you look more like a princess than a toad, but we can't have you exploding all over my nice dining room.'

'That's gross.' She giggled. 'Ouch.' She held her stomach. 'It hurts to laugh I'm so full.'

He stood up and held out his hand. 'Let's go for a stroll. The moon will be up soon and we'll walk our dinner down.'

They walked down the driveway and turned up the dirt road in the opposite direction to Savannah's farm, and she smiled when Theo took her hand to hold. Another thing she'd learned. He was a romantic.

Once their eyes had adjusted, it wasn't dark at all. The moon was still to rise but the sky was so clear it seemed the stars were enough to reflect off the road and allow them to see. There was a gentle breeze against her skin and the sudden sound of an owl made her jump. Benson jumped, too. He wasn't happy out in the dark and stayed close on her heels.

'Thank you for that wonderful dinner. You could be a chef instead of a doctor.'

'And you could be a farmer instead of a nurse.'

'I can do both.'

He squeezed her hand. 'So can I but not full time.'

She lifted her head, shaken out of her desultory thoughts. 'Are you trying to say I can't work on the farm and in the hospital—that I'm not doing either properly?'

'No, you're doing a great job, but come off it, Savannah. You're running yourself into the ground.'

She pulled her hand from his and stopped. 'I am not.'

He caught her hand and tucked it back into his. 'OK. It's your life. I'm just saying this as a friend of your uncle's.'

'Don't bring my uncle into it.' She had a thought.

Ha. 'You work full time and do the occasional night duty, and you have a farm,' she retaliated.

'Ah. But I don't have pigs and chickens. I only rent out the land for someone else's cattle. If the stock need care I inform the owners and they do the work.'

She shook her head. 'It didn't occur to me that you didn't have animals. That's not really a farm. It's a block of land.' She had another thought. 'You don't even have a dog!'

'I can't be tied down. And animals tie you down.'

'So do relationships, Theo. So what are we doing here?'

'We're walking down a road, bickering, and that's not how I planned on spending the evening.'

'How were you planning on spending the evening?' She couldn't help the sarcasm in her voice.

'Actually, I was going to challenge you to a game of Scrabble.'

She coughed into her hand and it sounded like she said, 'Liar.'

'Sorry? I didn't catch that.'

'Nothing.' She stopped and he stopped, too. 'Let's go back. How about I help you wash up and then you take me home.'

He shook his head at her. 'All this because I said you would run yourself into the ground doing two full-time jobs? That's carrying even your independence a bit far, surely.'

She almost got angry then and tried to pull her hand out of his again. He held on. She sighed and refused to be drawn into an undignified tug of war. She strove to establish a feeling of reason and calm but it was difficult, with Theo standing beside her. She made herself draw a deep breath and loosen her shoulders, and her head cleared. Was it carrying independence too far?

'OK. Let's go back and play Scrabble.' The mood lightened and they both relaxed in relief. He loosened his hold on her but she let her hand rest in his.

He rubbed his chin with his other hand. 'Now I'm flummoxed. I don't actually own Scrabble.'

'Fine. We'll go back and make mad, passionate love instead,' she teased.

The moon rose in the east and it was as if the whole landscape had suddenly had the light turned on. The road was a silver ribbon ahead and behind them. The fences stood out in the paddocks like black sentries. She just caught the wicked look in Theo's eye before he pulled her around to face the way they'd come and said, 'I'll race you back.'

She had to laugh. 'I'm not running anywhere, it's far too beautiful a night.'

They walked home to Theo's house and pretended they had no plans for when they got back.

Which was lucky as they heard the phone ringing as soon as they made it inside the door.

It was Dr Ross.

'There was an accident out at the airport ten minutes ago. We're expecting between ten and fifteen incoming casualties. I need you to go out and help with the triage station at the site. Thankfully we only service small airlines around here.'

'I'm on my way, and I'll bring Sister Laine with me.'

'That will save me a phone call. All speed.' And he hung up.

'What's happened?' Savannah could tell it was major.

'That was John Ross. Small commercial aircraft accident at the local airport. Grab your handbag while I get my kit. We'll drop Benson off and you can pick up a pair of trousers on the way. The skirt will probably hamper you.'

When they arrived at the airport, chaos had been there before them. The engine of the commuter aircraft had failed suddenly after take-off and the pilot had been attempting to circle the airstrip to land again, but the aircraft had fallen from the sky and scattered its frail human cargo.

The wreckage lay strewn across the outer perimeter of the airfield and the rotating beacons of the ambulance and fire-engines illuminated the scene in red strobe flashes.

The state emergency services were busy setting up extra lights and Dr Smythe and Julia were in the designated triage area. Both looked up at Savannah and Theo with unmistakable relief.

Dr Smythe wiped his brow. 'Way out of my league here, old son. The ambulance paramedics know what they're doing and are bringing the injured to this area for triage before transporting them.'

'You're doing a fine job, Paul. Who's left in Emergency to receive?'

'Dr Ross and Dr Hudson, but there's a full team

on the way up from Newcastle. Should be at the hospital in an hour.'

Theo glanced around at the half-dozen injured passengers and noted the coloured tags attached for easy identification of their priority in transport. Red for immediate attention, orange for serious, green for walking wounded—but he couldn't see any white tags, indicating a dead person, and prayed he wouldn't.

'Right,' Theo said briskly. 'You and Julia see to the orange tags, Paul. Re-tag if they deteriorate. Remember all non-urgent cases go out last. As long as they can travel safely, give them pain relief and transport them when we can. Savannah, stick with me.'

Savannah picked up a portable vital-signs monitor, tucked it under her arm and followed him. It was like something out of a horror movie. While nobody was hysterical, the suppressed moans of the badly injured were eerily horrific.

He moved to the nearest red-tagged patient and crouched down beside her. The plump, elderly lady held a blood-soaked bandage to her chest. Her lips were blue and her breathing was rapid and shallow.

'Hello. I'm Dr McWilliam. Sister is just going to take your blood pressure.'

Savannah knelt on the other side of the woman and gently checked that her arm was undamaged before she strapped on the cuff.

'Eighty on forty. Pulse one hundred and thirty-two.'

Theo gently lifted the bandage and grimaced. He squeezed the woman's hand and stood up. 'I'm afraid you need surgery. We'll get some blood volume expander into you and then you'll be transported to the hospital.' He turned to Savannah. 'Send her in the next ambulance. She has internal bleeding we can't help here.' He moved on.

Savannah delved into the packed-to-go disaster box that contained front-line medical supplies and connected up another flask of fluid to the woman's intravenous line.

The next free ambulance arrived and was directed to load and go. Savannah handed a small sheet of instructions to the driver.

'Keep up the IV as fast as you can run it. Theatres will be standing by for you when you arrive.' She squeezed the woman's hand in farewell.

Savannah caught up with Theo as he pulled a sheet over the face of an elderly gentleman who wouldn't suffer any more.

'White-tag him,' Theo said gruffly. Their eyes met in mutual distress but there wasn't time to wonder about the why of it all.

The third person red-tagged was a very young boy who moved restlessly on the ground. His breathing was laboured and his delirious speech was slurred. His mother was hugging his hand against her bloodied cheek and the tears ran down her face.

Savannah crouched down beside her. 'This is Dr McWilliam. We'll have your boy at the hospital as soon as possible.'

Theo knelt on the other side. His voice was gentle. 'How old is he?'

'Four. Five soon. Will he be all right?'

'We can only attempt to stabilise for transfer until we can get them to hospital. We'll try and have him there as soon as we can. I'll send him in the next ambulance and you can go with him.' He looked at Savannah. 'Torch?'

Theo lifted the boy's eyelids and held out his hand while Savannah scrabbled through the box until she found a slim neurological torch for Theo to check the reaction of the boy's pupils. The findings were grim.

'One pupil slightly larger than the other and reflexes slow.' He gently felt the back of the boy's head and his gloved hands came away with a smear of blood. 'Depressed fracture of the skull. Make sure they keep checking that left pupil. If it starts to blow he needs the pressure off his brain pronto. Next out and straight to Theatre.' He squeezed the green-tagged mother's shoulder. 'His head injury is dangerous and I'm afraid we can't help him here. But specialist surgeons are on their way.'

Another ambulance arrived and Savannah directed them to gingerly move the child onto a stretcher. 'This is the boy's mum. More care than speed, guys.' She quickly scribbled on his sheet and handed it over.

Theo's face was grey as he watched the small boy being wheeled away. 'I hope to heaven the Newcastle team brings a neurosurgeon.'

Savannah nodded. 'And soon.' She saw Theo turn away. 'Theo, are you all right?' She rested her arm on his sleeve and he turned to look at her. She could tell he wasn't seeing her.

'Theo! Let's move.'

He blinked and some of the colour came back into

his face. 'Sorry. It hit me for a minute. I know some-one that age.' Then he turned away to move mechan-ically to the next red-tagged patient.

Savannah nodded and briefly wondered who the child was. Obviously someone Theo was close to, judging by the emotion in his face. How would she feel if that were Greg's daughter, Amelia? Her stom-ach dived and she switched that thought off. She shook her head and frowned. No time for that now.

By one o'clock in the morning all the trapped pas-sengers had been released and transported. As Savannah handed the last injured passenger into an ambulance, she sighed. Her shoulders drooped as if someone had cut the strings on a puppet. Thank good-ness it was Saturday tomorrow. She smiled wearily—no, make that today!

'Tired?' Theo slipped his arm round her shoulders and hugged her. 'It's been a long day for you. The hospital has sent out some night staff to clean up here so we can leave.' He brushed a lock of black hair off her forehead. 'You're out on your feet. Let's go.'

She'd had the chance to watch Theo at work in the most difficult circumstances and his ability for quick assessment and diagnosis had awed her. 'You're skilled at coping in difficult conditions, Theo.'

He answered her but she got the feeling he didn't want to talk. 'I had a good assistant.' He shut the car door after her and walked around to the driver's side. 'Close your eyes and I'll wake you when we get to your place.'

She was tired. It felt like she'd shut her eyes for

only a moment before Theo's voice intruded. It seemed to come from a long way.

'Wake up, Savannah. You're home.'

She opened and shut her eyes a couple of times until they focused on the man standing beside the car. 'Sorry. I really did drop off.'

'That's fine. Give me your keys and I'll open your door for you.'

He held out his hand to help her out and she was glad of the support. Her legs seem to have refused to take her weight, but she persevered until she didn't need his help. 'It's OK. You go. I'll manage.'

Theo frowned and looked as if he was going to argue. 'Right. I'll see you tomorrow. Thank you for coming with me tonight,' he said formally, and walked back to his side of the car.

She unlocked her front door and waved as she watched his tail-lights go down the driveway. It had only been hours but it seemed like a week ago that she and Theo had been walking down the road in the moonlight.

CHAPTER EIGHT

SAVANNAH slept heavily and when she woke the sun was high in the sky. The pigs. It was amazing they weren't beating down her front door and screaming for food. She threw back the covers and padded through to the kitchen. There was a note on the kitchen table. 'Thought you'd sleep in. Pigs fed. See you later, Theo.'

She squashed the feeling about how special it felt that someone wanted to spoil her. That was how you became dependent on people. Theo was getting out of hand, and if she wasn't careful he'd be taking over her life.

She needed some space from him before she saw him next, and drove the forty minutes to the beach. She walked around the headland for a couple of hours and the salt air settled some of her disquiet. But it lacked that special pleasure because there was no one to share the moment with.

So why was she pushing Theo away?

Because last night she'd thought of Amelia and how much she missed her.

She'd survived the loss of Greg and his small daughter and now it was time to find a normal, responsible man. One who wanted to get married and have children. Children that Savannah could call her own and that no one could take away.

Children she would never walk away from.

* * *

'Theo, I am quite capable of managing my farm on my own.' Later that afternoon she'd been checking fences, brushing up on her horse-riding on Billy, when she came across Theo restringing wire through a corner post.

'It's a mutual boundary, Savannah, and I don't have to inform you when I repair my own fences.' He looked up at her astride the horse. 'At least I'm not building fences—why are you so determined to keep distance between us?'

'I'm an independent woman—it's my job to look after myself.'

'You're stubborn, and your load is too heavy for a single woman.'

'What do you want me to do, Theo? Marry you?' She felt the heat creep up her cheeks. Why on earth had she brought that up again? She muttered, 'Sorry.' Then wheeled the horse's head around towards home.

Billy obligingly took off up the bank and she felt the breeze cool her heated cheeks. She felt like an idiot.

The horse crested the hill and she leaned back in the saddle as he started down the other side towards the gully beside the house. She realised she wasn't even directing Billy as he headed for home. Lucky he was paying attention.

Just as they broke into a canter to pass a small outcrop of boulders at the bottom of the hill, Billy's ears flattened and he shied in terror at the hiss of a black snake they'd accidentally disturbed.

Normally a competent rider, Savannah's thoughts were still tangled back at the fence with Theo, and the sudden shift in direction from the horse took her by surprise. She felt herself fly from the saddle, the reins jerked out of reach. Luckily, her tangled foot flew from the stirrup as she fell.

Theo watched her ride up the hill away from him and swore softly under his breath.

No, he didn't need her to marry him. He didn't need another wife. He just wanted to be Sam's father. And Savannah's lover. He didn't want to push them both into something that might not work out.

His only sin had been to let Savannah know he could see her load was heavy. At least that was what he'd thought he'd been getting at.

She was as prickly as an echidna, puffing up with her spines as soon as he looked like exposing any of her weaknesses.

It wasn't weakness but a fact. It *was* too much for anyone to work full time and then single-handedly run a farm with a complete contingent of animals. And that included short, dark-haired sirens with boundless energy.

He hadn't liked the way she'd ridden up that hill.

He collected his tools and stowed them in the boot of his cruiser. She'd probably give him the cold shoulder, and he should really go home and not worry, but he'd just drive past and check she was OK.

When he saw Billy standing beside the stables, his sides heaving, with the reins dragging on the ground, the coldness of dread settled in his stomach and he swore again.

He steered his vehicle down the first gully until he

came to the start of the home flat. The whisky grass was long and waving in the afternoon breeze. He slowed to a crawl. If she'd fallen in here he'd have to be careful he didn't run over her.

He narrowed his eyes at the hill at the end of the flat. She would have come over the top and down this side near the boulder outcrop.

When he saw her lying on her back, so still in the grass, he felt the breath from his own lungs desert him. She had to be all right. He loved her. It was as if a ball of light exploded in his brain. How? When?

In the big picture it didn't matter. He wasn't going to lose her. Visions of all the quadriplegic tragedies he'd seen crowded his mind, and he squashed them fiercely. Not Savannah. Suddenly it was hard to open the car door.

But he had to switch off his emotions and become the doctor Savannah needed.

When Savannah regained consciousness, the back of her head was throbbing and her shoulder felt as if it were on fire. She gingerly wriggled her toes and the very ends of her fingers. She offered a silent prayer of thanks when all seemed to be working. She flexed her feet and her left hand but any effort to move the right side of her upper body sent bolts of pain to encourage her to leave well alone. It was bearable if she didn't move.

At first she didn't connect with how she came to wake up flat on her back in the thickly grassed paddock, but then it all came back. Billy. Theo. The horse shying. She hoped the snake which had made the horse shy had been as frightened as Billy and didn't come over to investigate.

Visibility was limited from where she lay. The grass was a good two feet tall and she'd made a flattened area with her landing. The rest blocked any view.

'Hell.' She congratulated herself on her control.

She hadn't been here long, as the sun harassing her headache didn't seem to have moved any further down the sky. Which meant Theo wasn't that far away but too far to hear her call. She'd have to get home herself.

She tried lifting her good shoulder, but as soon as any angle was achieved the right shoulder complained loudly and painfully. She sank back. She bit her lip to stifle a whimper. 'Bloody hell.' Not such good control but, in the circumstances, acceptable.

One of those inch-long brown ants crawled over her hand and she flicked it off with a shudder. She twisted her neck as much as she could and hoped she wasn't lying on an ants' nest. A shudder went through her system again.

Two more ants were coming her way. This wasn't amusing. She could feel the panic tightening her chest. She tried to wriggle sideways and the pain sent a red ball of flame through her shoulder. She froze.

Suddenly she realised it wasn't just the beating of her heart she could hear but a strange swooshing noise. The ground rumbled beneath her ear and then it stopped.

Theo's face blocked out the sky. He knelt down beside her and she had never been so glad to see anyone. 'Don't move, Savannah.' His eyes were fierce as he assessed the way she was lying.

Her voice was weaker than she'd expected. 'To the rescue again, Theo. Thank God.'

He rested his hand on her cheek and then ran his fingers down her arm. 'Can you move your toes and fingers?'

'Yes.' She watched his shoulders drop fractionally with his relief. 'I've hurt my arm and shoulder and I think I'm near one of those brown ant nests.'

'OK, sweetheart, I'll just check you over and get you out of here.' His hands were gentle as they skimmed her body, directing her to squeeze his hand, flex her foot and lift her good arm. He covered her eyes with his hand and then let the light back onto her face quickly.

'Slight concussion. Were you knocked out?'

'Only for a few moments, but I orientated quickly when I woke up.'

He stood up. 'Right. You have a dislocated shoulder, which should be easy to pop back in, and maybe a crack in the radius and ulna at the wrist. The rest of you seems fine but we'll check for fractures later. I'll get you something for the pain before I move you. Allergic to anything?'

Savannah's headache was throbbing, her shoulder on fire and she was starting to feel the lumps and sticks under her. 'Brown ants. One bit me as a kid. Not clinically allergic but they scare the life out of me.'

Theo smiled but it didn't reach his eyes. 'Of course. The ant phobia. Hang on, I have something for that.'

He reached inside his car and came back with a spray-can of personal insect repellent. 'Hold my handker-chief over your face and I'll make you unattractive to the male brown ant.'

She hid her face in the white cotton and he squirted the outline of her body to keep the travelling insects away. She sighed and realised she'd been holding her-self tense in every muscle. Her back settled onto the ground and even the pain in her head and shoulder improved now that she didn't have to worry about the ants. 'Thank you.' Her comment was fervent. 'You're a lifesaver.'

He smoothed the hair off her forehead. 'Proof. There really is something you're afraid of.'

It took Theo another half-hour to get Savannah comfortable enough to move. He'd given her a small dose of morphine, and at her request attempted to nudge the shoulder back into place. It went in easily and he could tell Savannah was much more comfort-able. He'd spent two years as an orthopaedic registrar before his divorce, and he'd been quite blasé about reducing dislocations.

But Savannah's had him sweating before he could do it. By the time he had her sitting up in the Range Rover, with her arm in a sling to support her shoulder, he could admit he would be glad to hand her over to another doctor at the hospital.

He felt every bump and jolt on the way to town, and the fact that she didn't complain made him ache even more. It wasn't much fun when you loved the patient.

*   *   *

Later that night, Savannah lay in a private room at Bendbrook Country Hospital. Her lower arm was bandaged for support but she hadn't broken anything. Theo was concerned about her having adequate pain relief and care, and had insisted she stay overnight under observation. But she wanted to go home.

'Deal with it, Savannah. You're staying. I'll run you home in the morning. And you're going to need help.' Theo glared at her and she glared back.

'I can manage.' She caught a glimpse of her mutinous face in the mirror above the dresser. She looked ten years old. Damn. How was she going to manage? 'I'm sorry, Theo. You're right. I'll ring my mother.'

'You're sorry?' He raised his eyebrows and picked up the pencil torch. 'An apology from Savannah?' He shook his head. 'Are you feeling OK? I'll just check your neurological signs.' He moved as if to check for a sudden onset of brain damage. She glared at him some more and he laughed back at her.

'Couldn't resist.'

'Terrific. Now the man has a sense of humour. That's enough. I've said I'll get some help.'

He stood up to leave. 'Until your mother comes I'm happy to do the animals for you. In fact, I can do them while she's here if it's not her forte. It doesn't hurt to ask. And you wouldn't have to marry me.'

As an exit line it was a winner. She'd hoped he'd forgotten her outburst at the fence. Lord, this had been a big week. Life was a little too exciting in a place that her friends had assured her she'd be bored! She knew she should phone her mother, but she couldn't face ringing her tonight.

Theo didn't sleep much that night as he examined the revelation of the day. He loved Savannah Laine. And he did want commitment. He wanted to marry her. Have more children. Bring Sam home.

This was a different love to the wild infatuation he'd had for Marie, so wild and false it had burnt itself out almost as soon as he'd found out what she was really like.

His feeling for Savannah was a warts-and-all kind of love. He knew she'd drive him crazy sometimes but he could handle that sort of crazy—and the making up would be worth it. He felt like he'd been the one woken by a kiss—except it had been Savannah's almost kiss-of-death that had woken him.

He had never been as relieved in his life as when he'd realised she would be fine after what could have been a tragedy.

Even in the hospital, when she'd been cross and sore and bandaged to the hilt, he'd desired her. 'Desired' was too weak a word. He lusted after her. He chuckled to himself. She made him feel like a hormone-ridden teenage boy—all hot and bothered. And she warmed his heart with her innate kindness.

That one night in bed together had been a revelation of its own. She'd been giving and open and unashamed of her luscious little body, and together they'd made magic.

But would she come to love him? Savannah was disquietingly independent. He admired her fierceness and determination to complete a task. The old Theo would have said she was too driven. But now he had started to understand her.

Her decision to take on her uncle's farm and a full-time job was typical of her. But he could help. He needed to make her see they could temper each other.

He loved her honesty about her own shortcomings, although he wasn't sure he quite enjoyed her honesty about his own faults.

The great thing was…she wanted a family. He could see the hunger in her for babies and young children. He had to believe she would love Sam, too, as if he were her own.

But for the moment she had to get better and he would go slow. She was more shocked after her accident than she realised and he needed to help her get over this before he thought of himself.

The next morning, Sunday, Theo collected Savannah from the hospital.

Theo drove her slowly home and bullied her into the recliner rocker. He could tell that the trip in the car had been painful, although she hadn't complained. She couldn't get comfortable in bed and he saw the rainbow bruising that extended over most of her back. She should still be in the hospital.

She looked like a half-crushed butterfly with a bandaged wing, he thought, and he wanted to curl her in his arms and protect her from the pain. There were dark circles around her eyes and the brown collar and cuff sling stood out darkly against the white of her shirt.

He stood with a glass of water in his hand until she'd taken the pain tablets. He should take her home with him but he knew she'd refuse. Then he frowned. Her mother should be here.

'Ring her now.'

'She'll be at church.'

'Try.'

'I'll do it when you've gone.'

She looked up at him and he could see the plea in her eyes to let it be. He sighed.

'I'll be back at lunchtime to see if you need anything. I think you should try to sleep after you've called your mother.'

'Thank you for bringing me home, Theo. And for being there for me. Again.' She paused but still he didn't leave.

She closed her eyes tightly, willing him to leave before the tears she'd been holding back broke through. She could feel the inner walls crumbling and prayed he would go.

When she opened her eyes he was gone. A minute later she heard his car start up and drive away.

Now that she had privacy the tears refused to come. Her head ached and the lump in her throat grew bigger.

Benson nudged her hand with his wet nose and she looked at his big sad eyes. That did it.

Great welling tears fell like huge raindrops after a drought. She leaned her head back against the chair and they ran down her face and soaked the sling where it joined her neck. Benson whined and poked his nose onto her knee and she cried harder. Benson started to howl and she sniffed and then a tiny smile tugged at the corner of her mouth. The tears slowed and finally stopped.

'Did I sound that bad?' She rubbed his head with

her good hand and his little tail cautiously wagged. At least her headache had receded slightly, with the release of her pent-up emotions. But everything else hurt. 'I need a tissue, mate.'

Savannah struggled to sit more upright and lever herself out of the chair one-handed. When she was standing she kept her hand on the back of the chair until the waves of dizziness receded. This was ridiculous. But—ridiculous or not—she was going to need help. She plucked the tissue box from the table and wobbled back to the recliner and the table Theo had set up beside it. She reached for the phone.

'Hello, Bridget?'

'Savannah, how lovely to hear from you. Are you well?'

The housekeeper's warm voice brought fresh tears to Savannah's eyes. 'Well, no, I'm not so good at the moment. Is Mother home?'

'She's still at church, dear. What's wrong?'

'I've had a fall from my horse and banged myself up a bit. I'm supposed to have someone with me for the next week and really don't know who else I could ask.'

'I wish I could come up there for you.'

'You know she wouldn't agree to you leaving her in the lurch. I was hoping you could both come.'

'I'll certainly make sure your mother understands you need her.' Savannah heard the lack of certainty in Bridget's voice. 'But there's an opening night at the local art gallery in three days and she'll be cross if she misses it. Perhaps after that?'

Savannah put the phone down. Her mother wouldn't come. If she were honest with herself,

Savannah would have to admit she didn't want anybody but Theo. She was frightened she was setting herself up for more disappointment and it smacked of becoming reliant on a man again. But he probably wouldn't want to come here either and she decided she wouldn't ask him.

When her mother rang back it was as she'd feared. 'You poor thing. What a nuisance for you. Can't you come to Sydney and be looked after? I'm afraid it's ridiculous to imagine me on a farm. I couldn't bear the trip either.'

Savannah understood. That was how she felt, too. The thought of sitting in a car or bus from Bendbrook to Sydney was unthinkable. What was she going to do? The trip with Theo from hospital to home had tried her strength.

'Not to worry, Mother. I'll survive and be quite self-sufficient in a week or so.'

'If you're sure, then. Hope you feel better soon.'

'Thanks.' Savannah hung up, her voice falsely bright. But what to do until then?

When Theo walked into Savannah's kitchen at one o'clock he couldn't believe his eyes. She was leaning against the bench. A two-litre plastic milk bottle was jammed in the drawer and she had a nutcracker in her left hand and was wrestling with the lid.

'You all right there?' he said with his eyebrows scraping the top of his forehead.

'The damn lid is stuck and I can't even make myself a coffee,' she said, and burst into tears.

He gathered her to him and cradled her. His hand soothed her forehead and he shushed her. 'It's OK, sweetheart. We'll manage.' He pulled her gently towards her chair and settled her into it. 'That's it. I'm staying until your mother comes.'

Savannah wouldn't meet his eyes. 'She's not coming.'

He'd had a feeling the land was going to lie that way. Actually, he was glad. 'Well, you're stuck with me, then.'

She rubbed her forehead with her good hand. 'I can't let you do that.'

'You don't have any choice for at least a week. Live with it.'

He went back to the kitchen and returned with her coffee. 'When was the last time you had some pain relief?'

She took the cup. 'Thank you.' She looked up. 'You gave me tablets before you left.'

He crouched down beside her chair and stared into her face. 'That's more than four hours ago.'

She nodded.

'And is your arm and back hurting and do you have a headache?'

She couldn't lie. 'Yes.'

He shook his head and stood up. 'If you were looking after someone, would you make sure they had adequate pain relief?' He answered his own question. 'Of course you would.' He reached for the tablets and her glass of water.

'This is doctor's orders. Take two Digesic four-hourly for the next forty-eight hours and then I may allow you to take them six-hourly. If, that is, I consider you're getting adequate pain relief. Do you understand?'

He wished he didn't have to work but there really wasn't anyone to replace him on such short notice. She'd have to rest for the next few days anyway and he'd be back for the nights.

She nodded. 'But I'll feel like such a wimp taking them and end up sleeping most of the day.'

He sighed. 'It's Sunday. Sleep. While you're sleeping your body's getting a chance to heal itself. You know that.' He tilted his head. 'Have you had lunch?'

'I was going to have some after the coffee.'

'Do you like corned beef? I brought some.'

She nodded.

'Pickles?'

She inclined her head again.

The sandwich, when it came, was precisely divided into four triangles on a plate with a napkin. She felt like a schoolchild, but it was sweet and she had to smile.

'Thank you, Theo.'

'I make a mean sandwich.'

He grinned back at her. What a gorgeous smile he had! It was doing strange things to her stomach—or maybe that was the painkiller kicking in! Come to think of it, she felt a bit light-headed. If she lived with Theo for the next week she'd either be in love or a basket case from trying not to be.

'Why don't you just drop in every now and then? I really hate putting you out like this,' she said.

She saw his mood change. 'You hate having to rely on anyone, you mean. What do you think I'm going to do, Savannah? Take advantage of you? You need to learn to trust people.'

He collected the empty plate and coffee-cup and

stared down at her. 'I *will* stay. You *will* rest and get better. *Then* I'll go home.' He caught her eye and he spoke slowly and clearly, as if to a child.

'Unfortunately, I have to work the next four days. So tomorrow Mrs Hawes, my cleaning lady, will deputise for me until I get home. I hope she'll prevent you from doing anything that will prolong this state of affairs you find so irksome.'

'That's not necessary.'

'I think it is. You're shocked and badly bruised so, please, don't fight me on this, Savannah.' He smiled without humour. 'Luckily, you'll see very little of me to start with.'

She hadn't meant to sound ungrateful and now she'd succeeded in annoying him. She sighed. She needed help, he'd offered, and she should consider herself fortunate not to be still struggling on her own.

'Fine. Thank you very much, Theo.'

She closed her eyes. Her head hurt, and it was easier to drift off with some painkillers on board. She didn't see his concerned frown or hear his muttered curse.

CHAPTER NINE

MONDAY to Thursday passed in a blur for Savannah.

Theo left at nine-thirty in the morning and came back at six-thirty at night. He'd been right. She saw very little of him, but she couldn't help treasuring the little time she did have with him. She hadn't realised he could be so good-natured.

Mrs Hawes was efficient but not talkative, and Savannah's house had never been so clean. She offered to help Savannah to shower and change in the afternoons, solving a problem Savannah had been worrying about. At least she was spared the embarrassment of asking Theo for that help.

As for payment, the barter system was employed. Mrs Hawes would help while Theo was working and do the farm chores before going home in the evening, in exchange for four of Savannah's medium-sized female grower piglets.

Savannah had hated the thought of sending any of her pigs to the meatworks and Mrs Hawes wanted to breed from them. Both women were happy with that.

Savannah's bruises grew darker but less painful and the swelling in her wrist gradually subsided to purple. Her shoulder almost never ached but her lower arm continued to throb if she overused it.

She could wander around a little but she hadn't realised how difficult everything was, single-handed.

She couldn't sweep or open a tin or even pull her jumper off herself for the first forty-eight hours. In the daytime, she mostly caught up on the sleep that eluded her at night.

Still uncomfortable lying in bed with all her bruises, she chose to remain tucked up in the chair in the lounge room. Naturally, it made sense for Theo to have her larger bed while she wasn't using it. Ha!

He treated her like a sister for the few hours they had together at night, checking her injuries, making a late dinner, watching television for an hour and then dropping a light kiss on her forehead and casually going to bed.

She spent most nights staring at the patch of star-strewn sky she could see through the window from the chair, while her mind replayed scenes from the night they'd slept in her bedroom together.

Once the lights were out, the thought of Theo asleep in her bed, his arm across her pillow, played havoc with her imagination. Even worse, not once did he look like he wished she were with him.

She had to admit he'd been incredibly easy to get along with—too easy for her peace of mind.

By the time she waved goodbye to Mrs Hawes on Thursday evening, Savannah was feeling a lot more self-sufficient.

If she took it slowly and used her brains, she could accomplish most things needed to look after herself.

She glanced at the clock. Theo would be home soon.

That had a strange ring to it. Theo would be home

for a whole three-day weekend soon—except that this wasn't his home. It was hers.

He didn't really live here and she needed to remember that.

But she couldn't help the butterflies at the thought of him here through the day with her for the next seventy-two hours. To be honest, now she was feeling stronger and less shattered, she was looking forward to seeing more of him.

Theo drove away from the hospital Thursday afternoon humming a tune. These last four days of going home to Savannah's, just knowing she was waiting for him, even reliant on him, had felt good. He enjoyed whipping up a meal for two instead of one, savoured her company and even the sweet vagueness she'd acquired since her fall. He'd even grown fond of the dishmop dog. And he'd hugged the knowledge to himself that he believed they had a future together.

She'd looked much stronger this morning and he couldn't help shaking his head at how quickly she was regaining her independence. He shouldn't have been surprised, though. She was tough.

She'd been reluctant to accept his help but she must see he could be relied on. He'd like to take her uncaring mother and shake some maternal duty into her as he began to realise how much it hurt Savannah to be ignored by the woman.

His life had finally taken a turn for the better. Even his lawyer had rung today and said the courts were apparently taking his side in his case to win custody of Sam.

He slapped his hand on the steering-wheel. He had to talk to Savannah about that as his avoidance of the subject smacked of lack of trust, although he was just unused to opening up to people. But it was time to let Savannah in.

When he drove up, Benson wagged his tail instead of barking and rushed onto the verandah to greet him. Savannah followed more slowly.

She thought he looked so tall and handsome and the type of man any woman would be proud to greet after work. He warmed her just by being there. When had that happened?

Theo raised quizzical eyebrows at the sight of Savannah and her dog as they waited for him.

'That boring a day, eh?' He dropped a kiss on her forehead and gestured for her to precede him inside.

Savannah wondered how they'd got into the home-from-work-kiss routine but agreed with the sentiment. Now that he was here she felt more alive than she had all day. The warning bells clanged as she acknowledged he would leave when she could manage.

Living on the tablets, it had made everything sweetly blurred around the edges. Now that she'd cut them back, she was more grounded and some of her excuses for letting him take control were beginning to look a bit lame.

'So, how is everything at the hospital?'

'We're managing.' He dropped a casual arm around her good shoulder and smiled down at her. 'You know, I think I even miss having you there.'

'That's because I'm very efficient.' She stepped out from under his arm. 'Speaking of efficient, Mrs

Hawes has been wonderful. Thank you for arranging her help, Theo. She's agreed to accept four of the older piglets in payment.'

He frowned but didn't say anything. Savannah suspected he'd intended to pay his housekeeper a wage while she'd cared for Savannah. Thank goodness it didn't look like he was going to fight about it.

She changed the subject and gestured to the candlelit dining room. 'Even a one-armed lady can set the table.'

His face cleared. 'And very clever she is, too.' He picked up the shopping bag he'd brought with him. 'Now, for tea I've brought some fillet steak and thought we'd go for steak Dianne. Does that meet with your approval?'

Savannah heaved a sigh of relief that the matter of Mrs Hawes had been dropped. She didn't want to fight with Theo but she wouldn't have him paying for her help. 'Well, I don't suppose I'll be breathing on anyone with my garlic breath. Sounds great.'

His eyes held a gleam of mischief. 'Later I hoped you'd think about breathing on me. It wouldn't matter if we both had garlic.'

'You wouldn't be propositioning one of the walking wounded, would you, Theo?'

'Only with great delicacy.'

The way he said 'delicacy' trickled rivulets of pleasure down her spine and she could feel the goosebumps popping up along her arm. How did he do that? She rubbed her good arm and kept her face averted to hide the confusion she felt. So he didn't think she was his sister after all!

And he was featuring as a large part of her life when she'd promised herself she wouldn't get involved. Because he didn't want commitment—did he?

She turned back at the sound of a cork being pulled from a wine bottle. She glanced at the expensive label.

'Merlot as well? What are we celebrating?'

'To your convalescence and maybe a weekend adventure together.' His face became more serious and he placed the wine bottle aside to breathe, before stepping closer. He slid his finger under her chin. 'And a new long-term understanding between us, I hope.'

His eyes caught and held hers. 'I care about you, Savannah, and I need you to think about how you feel about me.'

Savannah sat stunned by his sudden declaration. He'd been very caring, of course, over the last few days, but more brother-like than lover-like. Of course, she'd been away with the fairies half the time on the analgesics.

But she hadn't been good enough for her mother. Greg and Amelia seemed to have managed to forget her pretty easily. What if Theo got tired of her, too? Wasn't it better to keep it light than start to think permanence—because that was when it really hurt to be let down.

She sighed and hated her own insecurities. 'What if I'm scared that it's not going to work out? What's wrong with what we have at the moment?'

'Apart from me sleeping in your bed without you—which I really hate—I enjoy your company. I think we could be good together. I think we could get even better. In fact, I think we could be winners all round.'

He took his finger from her chin and stroked it down her cheek. She could hear the tenderness in his voice and she swallowed the prickly thickness in her throat.

'Just think about it. I'm not going to rush you. Let's enjoy our long weekend together first.' Then he kissed her and she forgot to worry for the moment. They fitted together so perfectly and she felt so secure as he held her in his arms.

Later, after dinner and most of the wine, they agreed to swap stories. She told him about the loss of a father she couldn't remember and the reality of a mother who often forgot she had a daughter.

'She doesn't mean to be unkind. She just lives in a bubble. Luckily, if I'm careful, Daddy's money will keep her immune from the realities of life. I've arranged that everything is paid automatically, found her a lovely housekeeper who will keep everything running and a solicitor who will ensure she doesn't end up penniless. You know the saying—my mother is one of those travel agents that deals in guilt trips, and it's nice to get away from the daily wallow in remorse.' She shrugged.

'I'm useful to have around if there's a problem and I've learnt to shrug off her lack of parental love. But I know, for other people at least, it does exist. I found it on holidays here with my aunt when she was alive and later Uncle Andy, so I'm luckier than some. And I'm trying hard to not let it affect me. If I ever have children, they'll know what a mother's love is.'

Theo squeezed her hand but he was wondering how anybody could not love her.

She turned her face to look at him. 'Tell me about you.'

He stared into the past. 'Well, I had plenty of love in my childhood. My parents spoiled me until they both died in a road accident when I was eighteen.'

'It must have been hard to lose both of them.'

He nodded. 'I felt like someone had taken an axe to my whole life and parts of me were just hacked off. That's when I decided I'd become a doctor. I was ready to go to uni and it gave me direction to have a goal.' He squeezed her hand. 'I think it would be harder to not have love at all than to lose it.'

He could see Savannah thought he was talking about her childhood, and he was, as well as Sam's. He glanced out of the window as if to see a far-away place. He was thinking about what Sam was missing out on now. At least he, Theo, had had both parents who'd loved him for all of his childhood.

He refocussed on Savannah's face and realised she'd asked him a question.

'Why did you come back here to live? Your parents only came here on holidays, or when your father wanted a break from the city. I remember Uncle Andy saying that if he were rich like your dad he'd stay here all year.'

'My mother wasn't keen on country life. But she put up with it a couple of times a year because my father enjoyed it. In the end they bought a house at Blue Mountains which was half country and half city. But I always felt most at home here.'

Savannah changed the subject. 'You got married, Theo. What happened? Did you live here?'

He laughed, but there was no humour in it. 'The mistake of my life. She refused to even visit because the tar road ran out before we got here.'

'You must have loved her once.'

He glanced out of the window again and forced himself to remember the way of it. 'I was young, alone and fell in love with the dream of what I thought she was. I was a fool and she lied and cheated the love out of me very quickly.'

He read the sympathy in her eyes but he didn't deserve it. He'd been stupid and Sam had been the victim. He drew a deep breath to tell her about his son.

Savannah squeezed his hand. Poor Theo. The thought of Greg brought more loss. Three-year-old Amelia would have loved it here. But she had her proper mummy back now and she didn't need her Aunty 'Vannah any more.

Savannah tamped down the hurt she felt when she acknowledged how gullible she'd been.

If she hadn't been so aware of her thirtieth birthday approaching, maybe she wouldn't have been so quick to become involved. But she'd never found the soul mate she'd been looking for and she'd been starting to wonder if he was really out there.

Greg and his daughter had entered her life two years ago and had offered the chance to find the family she'd longed for. He'd said his daughter had lost her mother, and she'd believed him. Some tragedy he hadn't wanted to talk about.

Savannah had cared deeply for them both. There had been no stars in the sky when they'd made love but there had been no pits of darkness either. Savannah had been well satisfied with their life together and had nurtured Amelia as if she'd been her own.

In hindsight, she could see she'd been useful as a babysitter when Greg had had to work late, and as a partner she'd been inexpensive. She hadn't complained that as a couple they'd rarely gone out. And when he'd asked her to marry him one day she'd agreed that an engagement ring was an extravagance they could do without. They were saving up for the future.

Savannah smiled without humour. His and the real mummy's future, as it turned out. A mummy that had decided to come back from the dead.

Savannah shuddered at the memory of Amelia's mother walking in and saying it was time they were a family again. She remembered she'd looked at Greg to explain the madness and he'd blustered that he hadn't actually said his wife was dead. Savannah had walked away and hoped the adults would think of the child first next time around.

Theo was waiting patiently for her to come back to him. She blinked. 'I'm sorry. Pathetic memories. Someone lied to me, too. More by inference really. He was a doctor, like you. Except he had a three-year-old daughter and he wasn't coping well. I don't know where I got the impression his wife had died but I know he didn't disabuse me of the idea.'

She grimaced. 'Anyway, to cut a long story short,

we talked about marriage. I took over the mother role and the wife role without the ceremony, and worked with him to save for a mortgage. Then one day his real wife came back. She wasn't dead at all. And I had been the other woman without even knowing it.' She gave a harsh laugh. 'But, boy, was I useful for the time I was there. No wonder I wanted to come here and be responsible only for myself.'

CHAPTER TEN

THEO'S gut clenched. Hell. Fate must be lying on its back, hysterically laughing at him. So now what did he do? Say, 'I'm sorry to hear that—how about you help mind my son?' What if Savannah felt it wasn't her he wanted but a babysitter?

He sighed. He had to convince her he loved her. Before he told her about Sam. It would have to wait another day or two. And his love grew each time she revealed more of herself to him.

He leaned across and brushed her cheek with his lips. 'Are you tired?' He gently stroked the warmth of her fingers. 'How's your arm? The circulation's good even without the sling.'

She smiled at his shop-talk and he saw himself in her eyes. What did he look like to her? He could feel that buzz she gave him and he fought to quell his arousal. She'd been hurt and she needed rest—not love-making.

He ran his hand down her spine. 'Can I see your bruising?'

She looked at him from under her lashes and the warmth grew hotter. 'Is that like asking to see my collection of stamps, sir?'

He grinned and brought his hand back up to caress her neck. 'I think I'd better just look tonight.'

'My bruises. Hmm. If you can get to them under

153

this shirt.' She sighed, closed her eyes and relaxed into his hand as his fingers rubbed her neck and then slid down her back.

'Show me.' He undid the buttons of her shirt and she felt it loosen across her breasts.

He pushed the material off her shoulders and down her arms and still she kept her eyes closed to savour the sensation. Her body felt like soft clay beneath his fingers and the resonance of his strokes buried deeper into her belly. She couldn't help the soft groan, almost a purr, that slid out and she felt him drop a whisper of a kiss on her lips.

'Poor baby.' He tilted her back towards him and whistled softly between his teeth.

Today, in the mirror, she'd seen that it was still livid but more yellow than purple now. She opened her eyes and saw the concern on his face. 'It's getting better.'

Theo shook his head and kissed the darkest areas in sympathy. Then he kissed her neck.

His eyes darkened. 'You smell wonderful.' He bent and skimmed her skin with his lips like a dragonfly over water, and she felt the erotic tug deep inside from watching him inhale her scent as if it were the finest perfume.

His voice was rich with desire. 'I wasn't going to ask you this, but if I was very gentle and delicate, do you think I could take you to bed and try to take your mind off your injuries?'

Savannah lifted his hand to her lips and kissed his fingers. 'I do like the sound of delicate. But it's pretty hard work getting me out of all these clothes.'

'I'm sure it will be worth it—to see you feeling more comfortable, that is.'

'Right. I knew that was what you meant.'

Savannah woke with a smile next morning. Theo was watching her from the edge of the bed.

'Considering you only had half a woman to work with, you achieved great things last night, Dr McWilliam.'

The smile he gave her made her blush. He placed a spray of jacaranda blossoms on her pillow. 'You look particularly beautiful this morning.' He leaned across and brushed her lips with his.

He was looking at her as if he cared. The thought brought tears to her eyes and she pulled the sheet up to cover herself. To cower behind a barrier.

But he wouldn't let her. 'Look at me. Savannah?'

She raised her eyes and his were filled with understanding and something at the back of them that she was too frightened to name.

'Don't hide from me. Will it frighten you if I say I love you?'

She looked away then back at him. 'That's very sweet, but people don't have to say that because they sleep together.' She pleated the sheet. 'Don't say that, Theo,' she pleaded.

She could hear the smile in his voice. 'I found out I loved you the day you fell off Billy, Savannah. I couldn't imagine coping if I lost you before I'd even realised that I'd found you.'

Her eyes skittered away. 'Love is an easy word to say and a hard thing to live up to, Theo.' She dropped the wad of sheeting she'd mangled. 'I thought you weren't going to rush me?' But a part of her couldn't help daring to hope.

He squeezed her shoulder. 'I'm patient. Just think about it.'

Theo didn't mention it again but he showed it in many ways. The weekend flew by with gentle walks, wonderful food and shared laughter as they worked together on the farm. Theo did the bulk of the work and Savannah enjoyed watching the sheen of sweat he worked up on her behalf.

By Sunday night, a weekend of cosseting had healed her in body and spirit. She discarded the sling and her bruises weren't painful. The soreness from her shoulder was almost gone.

Again, this valley had given her warmth and caring as it always had. Only this time it had been Theo who'd showered the gifts. Her man. It was time to open her heart and trust again.

Theo had left for work half an hour ago and Savannah was still in her satin pajamas, leaning on the rail with a smile on her face.

Benson barked and at first she thought Theo had forgotten something, but the late-model coupé that turned into her driveway wasn't familiar. Wishing she'd had time to change, Savannah threw a wrap over her shoulders and went out onto the verandah as a woman stepped from the car.

She had long black hair, the palest complexion Savannah had ever seen and her lips matched the scarlet nail polish on what had to be cosmetic nails.

Savannah wondered how she managed not to break them.

'Can I help you?'

'Good morning.' The tone was friendly and her voice softly husky. At first Savannah thought she must be lost.

The woman smiled a soft self-deprecating smile. 'My name is Marie McWilliam and I'm looking for my husband, Theo. They mentioned at the hospital he could be contacted here.' She glanced up at Savannah with one of those I-hate-to-bother-you looks.

Savannah's stomach dropped and she felt the blood drain from her face. Not again.

Greg's wife had said something along those lines. She supposed she should be glad that Theo had told her there was an ex-wife in the wings. One who apparently had lied and cheated. Wasn't that what they all said? But if Savannah had loyalty it had to lie with Theo.

Savannah schooled her expression to polite interest. 'Good morning. You've just missed him. You could try at the hospital as he'll be there until at least six tonight.'

Strangely, the woman didn't seem particularly interested in finding Theo and continued to smile at Savannah. 'So he's mentioned me to you, then?' She raised thin, painted-black eyebrows.

Now, that was a little less angelic. Savannah frowned. 'No. Just that he was divorced. Is there anything else I can do for you?'

The woman turned to get back in her car but paused

at the open door. 'If you see him before I do, tell him Sam's missing him.'

Why would Savannah see him first? Wasn't the woman going to the hospital? 'I thought you said you're Marie?'

The woman gave a tinkling laugh. 'I am Marie. Sam's in the back of the car. He's the son Theo walked out on and I think it's about time we all became a family again.' She slid back behind the wheel and started the engine.

Now, what did that remind her of? Savannah could only stare, stony-faced, after her.

Savannah felt the cold of desolation seep into her and she felt sick as she watched the car bump down her driveway.

Theo had deserted his son? A son he hadn't mentioned to her. She shook her head. He wouldn't do that. Not the man of yesterday that she'd been almost ready to admit held her heart in his caring hands.

When she'd first met him, how many times had Theo told her he didn't want commitment? Having a child was a commitment and you didn't shirk that responsibility. It was an unpalatable thought.

How would he act when she gave him the message? How could any parent not care if their child missed them?

Greg's wife had seemed to have managed to leave Amelia while it had suited her. And what about Savannah's own mother? But not Theo. She hoped not Theo.

It was a lose-lose situation for Savannah. If Theo went back to his wife—make that ex-wife, but still mother of Theo's son—Savannah wouldn't stay on the sidelines.

If he didn't—if he refused to try and remake the family his son needed—then Savannah would have to accept he was just like her mother. How did she end up in these situations?

It had been a week yesterday since her fall from Billy. In one week she'd fallen in love and become the other woman yet again.

She leant her head against the verandah post. She'd ask Mrs Hawes if she wanted the rest of the litter in return for caring for the animals for another week, and she'd catch the Sydney bus to her mother's. Who cared if it was running away? She slapped the pole and it stung her tender arm.

Theo had a son. *Why* hadn't he told her? There had been plenty of opportunities for him to do so. Little pieces of the puzzle fell into place. The child that had been the same age as the boy with the head injury. Most probably the out-of-bounds room in his house belonged to Sam. The Coco Pops cereal packet from the guest who'd never come.

Yet they were all pointers to Theo missing his child, not deserting him. But why wouldn't he have told her?

Because he'd chosen not to. She felt lied to by omission. He had the same faults as the last man she'd trusted. She rubbed her brow. Did she wear a big sticker on her forehead that proclaimed SUCKER?

She wouldn't run yet. She'd stay for the moment. To stay and hear Theo's version—she at least owed him that.

*　　*　　*

Savannah spent the day worrying over the ramifications like Benson worried his bones. But she still couldn't see any change in the fact that Theo hadn't mentioned his son to her. When had he planned to tell her? The clock drew closer to the time Theo would come home.

She couldn't believe it when the woman's car turned into her gate at six o'clock that evening.

This time Savannah made out the small figure in the child seat.

It looked like she wouldn't be hearing Theo's version without the benefit of his ex-wife's presence. Savannah drew a deep breath and went out onto the verandah to see what she wanted. Sometimes it felt as though there weren't any more blows that could be dealt her.

'They were too busy for Theo to see me when I called at his work. I hope you don't mind if we wait here to catch him.'

Seeing that Theo was living at her house, doing her a favour, Savannah couldn't think of any objections. Personal preferences aside. 'No problem. Would you like a cold drink, lemonade or a cup of tea? It's very pleasant on the verandah.'

'That's very kind of you. Lemonade would be wonderful. It's such a disgusting road. I feel like I'll never get all this dust off me.' Marie shuddered.

She gestured to the child to get out of the car and Savannah couldn't see any great maternal outpouring from Marie. In fact, she reminded Savannah of her own mother. Immaculate and immune to what a child really needed.

The little boy crawled across the seats, slid out of the driver's side and stood behind his mother, holding onto the hem of her skirt.

Marie brushed his hand off and straightened her skirt. 'I've told you not to do that. Come and have a drink.'

Savannah winced at the memory of her own mother doing the same thing to her. At least Savannah's mother had smiled while she'd said it.

'Please, can I play with the puppy?' The soft voice had a tiny lisp.

He'd spied Benson. His mother scrutinised the offending creature. 'Does your dog bite?'

Savannah decided she definitely didn't like Theo's ex-wife. 'Well, he has teeth and can hold a bone. But I've never seen him attack anybody, if that's what you mean.'

'Very well. Come on, Sam. We'll wait for Daddy up here.'

Savannah tightened her fingers on the rail. That was it really. Theo was this child's daddy, the mother wanted a reunion and Savannah wouldn't stand in the way of that. Whatever was best for Sam.

She looked at him as he followed his mother onto the verandah. A miniature Theo but with black hair. He raised his hand to catch his mother's skirt again and then pulled back as if he'd remembered he wasn't allowed to.

Savannah's heart went out to him. He was very pale, as if he saw very little sun, and his thin wrists and arms looked fragile. But she could see his father in him. In his beautiful dark blue eyes and determined little chin.

Savannah brought out some glasses and set them on the verandah table. 'Please, sit down. I'll be back. I've a big bottle of lemonade, if I can get the lid off it.'

By the time she got back from the kitchen, Marie had settled into a chair and lit a cigarette. Up close, Savannah could see the fine pinch lines around her mouth.

Feeling like a bitch, she couldn't help being pleased the woman had some imperfections. Sam was sitting on the floor and had already made friends with Benson, which was a record as the dog usually avoided visitors.

Marie blew a stream of smoke at Savannah. 'So, why is Theo staying here at the moment?'

Straight to the point. Savannah mentally shrugged. She had nothing to hide. 'I fell off my horse last week and am only just returning to self-sufficiency. He's been very generous with his time.' Before the woman could ask anything else, Savannah took hold of the conversational ball.

'So, if the three of you become a family again, I assume you would move to Theo's house up the road.'

'When, not if, my dear,' Marie drawled, 'but I shouldn't think so. Sam starts school next year and I'm sure Theo would want him to receive a decent education.'

Savannah hated that. It was the same with the big hospitals. They thought no one could meet their standards. It was a mentality she'd met before. 'Really? I understand the local schools are of a very high standard. In fact, last year's top student in the state came from the local high school here.'

Marie raised her eyebrows sceptically. 'Indeed. How interesting.' She shrugged. 'But I'm not travelling on these roads for the rest of my life, anyway. No, we'll be returning to the city. Theo has a lovely home in Brighton-Le-Sands which he bought before the property market soared. Glorious bay views. I never could understand why he chose to live here like a navvy.'

'So you don't live there?'

'No.' She pursed her lips in annoyance. 'I asked for it in the settlement but only received tenancy rights at the Blue Mountains property that belonged to his parents. It's an even bigger house, but that's no use to me as it's entailed to Sam.' She laughed gaily. 'Theo bought me off with money.

'But I do think we should start again. It would be so much better for Sam to know his father and, to be honest—' she lowered her voice, presumably so Sam wouldn't hear '—Theo doesn't make the effort to see his son at all. So I've decided to do something about it.'

Savannah felt sick. The woman was obnoxious but Theo avoiding his own son wasn't much better. They probably deserved each other but Sam didn't deserve either of them. She had to get away from the woman. 'Do you mind if I take Sam down to see the chickens?'

'My heavens, don't tell me you do the whole farm

thing? How quaint. I suppose you have cows and pigs as well?'

'Most farms do.' Then she thought of Theo's. His didn't. But, then, he didn't want commitment.

Marie pulled out her lipstick case and mirror and checked her lips. 'I'll stay here but, by all means, take him. He'd probably love it.' She screwed her nose up. 'Little boys are so earthy.'

Savannah crouched down beside Sam as he patted a slavish Benson. 'Would you like to see the chickens and maybe the pigs I have down the yard before Daddy comes?'

He didn't meet her eyes, but he stood up and offered her his hand. 'Yes, please.' His diffident little voice made Savannah want to cuddle him to her. But she only squeezed his hand slightly and they set off. Benson even decided to come with them.

'My daddy has a farm.' His thin little arms swung as they marched down the driveway.

Savannah smiled. 'Yes, I know. And a lovely house, too.'

He screwed his nose up. 'Mummy's got a house. Houses aren't any fun. Farms are fun. Do your chickens have names?'

'No. But the pigs do.'

They spent a lovely half-hour meeting the animals, and she felt her own smile every time his childish laugh rang out.

On the way back, Savannah stopped on the house paddock side of the road and listened to the sound of a vehicle approaching. It sounded like a log truck. The heavily laden vehicles ponderously took up most of the narrow dirt road and were often a startling surprise to find around one of the many bends.

'Would you like to wait here and see a big truck? It makes lots of dust, though.'

The truck hurtled around the corner on its way to the timbermill in town. There was a huge cloud of swirling dust behind it and the noise thundered down on them. Sam put his hands over his ears but then the driver lifted a hand in a wave and tooted the horn.

A huge grin split the boy's face and he waved back.

'I'd like to drive a truck,' he said. They both smiled as they waved the dust away from their faces.

'I have to be careful when I drive out of my driveway because he's much bigger than my car. They usually come at this time of the afternoon.'

'Can we wait for the next one?'

'No. Your daddy will be home soon. We'd better go back to your mum.'

Sam slipped his hand into Savannah's. 'Is Daddy's car bigger than the truck?'

'I'm not sure about his car, but your daddy is bigger than the truck driver.'

Sam giggled and it changed his whole serious young face again. Savannah bit her lip. How could Theo bear not to see this child?

She looked down the road at the sound of another vehicle approaching. 'I think this might be your daddy now. Let's see how big his car is.'

Theo's Range Rover appeared around the corner, turned into Savannah's driveway and jerked to a halt. Theo threw open the door and with great strides reached his son and lifted him up to hug him. He cupped the back of Sam's head in one big hand and patted his back with the other, and spun him around.

Savannah felt the prickle of tears at the back of her eyes and chewed her lip. This was *not* a man who didn't care about his child. She sighed. She was glad about that.

'Sam? How can you be here?' He dropped a kiss on the boy's cheek. 'Daddy missed you.' Without waiting for the boy to answer, he turned to Savannah. 'Is Marie here? I'm sorry, Savannah, I should have told you sooner. This must have been a shock to you, and heaven knows what Marie's told you.' He glanced up at the house and his gaze hardened.

'Jump in the car, and I'll explain it all later.'

Savannah shook her head. 'You go ahead with Sam. I'll be up in a while.'

He frowned and she could see his impatience. 'It's not like that. I have very little to say to Marie. Come up with me.'

'No, Theo.' She looked at the boy in his father's arms. 'Discuss it with your family first.' And she walked back down to the sheds.

Theo cuddled Sam close as he watched the woman he loved walk away. The old Theo would have beaten his chest and blamed Marie for ruining his life yet again.

The new Theo refused to accept that his life was ruined. He had his son in his arms and that made the day a brighter one. But he wasn't going to lose Savannah either. He set his jaw and turned towards his car.

'Let's go see Mummy, Sam.'

Sam's thin arms were around his father's neck. 'I like that lady, Daddy. She showed me her pigs and they're funny.'

Theo looked down at his son's face, so similar to his own. It was wonderful to see him. 'Savannah is my special friend and I'm glad you like her. Now, slip across the seat and we'll drive up to the house.'

He started the car and drove the short distance to park beside Marie's car. She'd bought herself another two-door sporty number. He'd lost count of the cars she'd owned. No wonder she kept running out of money. His money. The next few minutes would be interesting.

He stepped onto the verandah. 'So, Marie. To what do I owe the pleasure of this visit?'

'Theo, darling. Sam and I have missed you.' She flowed up out of the chair, all thin and elegant and painted, and draped her arms around his neck.

He stiffened and took her wrists to pull them away. Then he dropped her hands and stepped back, finally immune to the practised spell she liked to weave.

'I've missed Sam, too.' His meaning was clear.

She pursed her lips petulantly. 'Don't be difficult, Theo. Enough of these strategies. I admit I've been playing games myself, but it's time we were a family again.'

'You never cease to amaze me, Marie. Have you run out of money once more?'

'I don't want your money, Theo. You want Sam and I want to go back to being a doctor's wife in Sydney. We can both have what we want if you stop being stubborn.' She stared up at him and he could almost accept that she believed what she was saying.

He looked at his son and then at his ex-wife. 'You're too late, Marie. You'll always be Sam's mother but I *will* gain custody of Sam. Personally, I've finished with you for good. I don't love you and the three of us will never be a family again. I'm sorry if you wasted a trip.'

He glanced up the valley. 'You'd better get going or you'll drive in dust all the way to town behind this log truck that's coming. You'll be hearing from my lawyer.'

Savannah just wanted to hide in the sheds and not hear the reasons why Theo and his family should be a unit again. The pain of that thought clamped around her chest and her eyes misted. What was she going to do? Run? Again? Like after her relationship with Greg?

She dashed her hands across her eyes. But she hadn't really loved Greg.

If she pulled out her heart and looked at it, the truth was there in indelible letters. She loved Theo.

He said he loved her. Did she believe him?

Savannah remembered his warmth and caring and, yes, love that he'd showed her over the weekend.

What about how she'd felt this morning before meeting Marie and Sam? Being with Theo, she'd experienced some of the most wonderful times in her life. He was the elusive home she'd been searching for. She didn't want to lose that or the sense of belonging she'd felt with Theo.

Ironically, she'd worried about his avoidance of commitment and yet she'd taken the first real obstacle and used it to avoid commitment herself. He deserved more than that.

She didn't want to lose the man she'd come to love by being frightened. He was worth fighting for.

He'd better really want to make a new life with her because she was going to fight for that love and win.

She stood up. He'd asked her to come up to the house with him—and she'd refused. It was time to stand by her man.

Savannah heard Marie's car start.

The sound of another log truck travelling into town vibrated in the air. She remembered Sam's delight when the driver had blown the horn. He was a sweet kid.

She looked up at the house. Marie had better leave now or she'd be eating the truck's dust all the way to town. The car hadn't moved from the house. Nope, she wasn't going to make it. And there was nowhere to overtake. She might as well stay for another half-hour until the dust settled.

Savannah could see Theo pointing to the direction of the truck's approach and then he was standing alone as Marie's car revved up and then shot down the driveway and straight out into the path of the on-coming giant truck.

Savannah's mouth dropped open in shock. Nobody could be that stupid. The woman was criminally insane to do it with her own son inside the car. Savannah held her breath and even thought Marie was going to make it for a moment as the log truck driver slammed on his brakes.

CHAPTER ELEVEN

THERE was a huge hiss of air brakes, a blast from the truck's horn and then the sickening sound of metal rending metal as the bull bar of the truck pushed the car in front of it, rolled the smaller vehicle like a beetle on its roof then back on its wheels and fired it off the road in front of it. The car ended up jammed between two trees—but anything was better than under the truck.

The next few minutes were burned in Savannah's brain as she dived into the dust-laden air. She raced past the end of the truck, along its length and around the front of the cab.

The driver was still sitting in the cab and she could see his trembling even as she passed. There really wasn't that much damage to the truck. He'd done well to stop so quickly and not lose his load onto Marie's car.

The coupé hadn't been so lucky.

Savannah kept running. She thought she was moving fast but Theo passed her as if she were standing still.

The rear of the car was completely smashed in but most of the impact had been on the passenger side and the roof. As she stopped she gulped in a breath. The smell of petrol hit her nose and she heard the drip, drip of liquid hitting metal ominously.

Both sides of the rear of the car were slotted between two trees and they couldn't see into the back seat. Theo moved to the bonnet to peer inside.

Incredibly, Marie appeared unhurt, fumbling with her seat-belt buckle and screaming for Theo to get her out. She had a thin trickle of blood running down her forehead and there was long crack across the front of the windscreen. Savannah clambered down into the ditch beside him. The driver's door was buckled and jammed shut, but the window was no match for Theo's desire to get to the occupants.

Theo pulled his shirt from his back and wrapped it around his fist. He smashed his fist against the glass and it shimmered into a thousand small cubes.

His face was a grim mask and Savannah knew what control he must be exerting on himself not to panic before he could get to his son.

'She looks OK to move.' He shot a glance at Savannah. 'Safer to get her out than wait.' He leaned in through the hole he'd made. 'Marie, can you move both legs all right?'

She was waving her arms around frantically so he didn't have to ask her that.

'Yes. Get me out!' Her voice was shrill and Savannah couldn't help noticing she hadn't asked about her son.

Theo enlarged the hole, swept glass beads everywhere, jammed his shirt over the window-frame and then leaned in to grasp his ex-wife's wrists. Marie slid through the opening, scraping her elbows and knees, but soon stood safely out of the car. She tumbled into his arms, screaming hysterically.

Savannah couldn't help the bitter observation that obviously she was all right. Theo tried to disentangle her arms from around his neck.

'Marie, stop yelling. You're out and Sam is still in there. Let me go.'

Savannah stepped up. 'Here. Give her to me while you get Sam.' Marie was more like an octopus than a woman as they extricated Theo from her grasp with great difficulty. Savannah felt like shaking her.

She dragged her by the arm, but it was hard to be gentle when Marie was fighting against her. They finally made it over to the side of the road and Savannah had to force Marie to sit down on the dusty grass. 'Stay there. I need to help Theo get Sam out.'

There were tears and dust and blood on Marie's face and her face was ashen. 'You can't leave me. I'm bleeding.' She wiped her forehead and gazed in horror at the blood on her fingers.

Savannah used every inch of her training not to allow her own emotions get the better of her. She enunciated slowly and carefully, 'Sit there. Put your head down on your knees and take some deep breaths. You're in shock. You've hit your head. If you stand up, you may faint. I must help Theo rescue Sam.'

She walked away and breathed out to regain control. For a moment she'd wished she'd been a man and could have spat the unpleasant taste of the woman's self-centredness out of her mouth. But she'd give her the benefit of the doubt. The woman was in shock and couldn't see her own behaviour.

Theo had tried to pull himself in through the side window but the shape of the car had changed to a diameter less than the width of his shoulders behind the front seat.

'Sam? Sam?' The urgency in Theo's voice lifted Savannah's pulse rate.

The tiny space occupied by Sam's car seat seemed ominously small for a child to survive in. They could barely see him amidst the tangle of seats, caved-in roof and twisted metal. What they could see was the boy's head hanging limply and his body slumping forward against the restraining straps.

Savannah touched Theo's shoulder. 'Let me try and slide in around the front seat.'

'Your arm isn't strong enough and you won't fit.' His lips were a thin line and his hands clenched at his sides as if he wanted to tear the metal apart with his own hands.

'The truck driver will have rung for a rescue unit and they'll bring all the equipment. They'll be at least thirty minutes. We need to cut open the roof and lift him out. It's too small for you to wedge yourself in there. And dangerous. The damn thing could catch fire at any moment.'

Theo didn't look like he would last thirty minutes but he wasn't letting her try. 'I can't let you endanger yourself, Savannah.'

Savannah's eyes narrowed. 'I'll get the fire-extinguisher from the shed and you can damn well stop the car burning. But I can try going in through the back window.' She ran back to the pig sheds.

Theo and the driver looked after her and then beat their way through the roadside vegetation to the rear of the car. They shattered the glass in the rear window and raked the beads away to enlarge the opening. Savannah skidded to a halt beside them and handed an old extinguisher to the truck driver. The driver looked up with new determination.

'I've a better one than this in the cab. Sorry, my brain's scrambled.'

Savannah took a deep breath and tucked her shirt into her trousers. 'Feel free to keep both of them on hand.'

Theo put his hand on her shoulder. His voice was rough as he forced himself to say it. 'You may be risking your life when it's too late.'

She brushed his cheek. 'Neither of us believes that. Now, lift me so I can slide in head first. Once I'm inside I should be able to see him even if I can't move him. At least I'd be able to feel his pulse and touch him.'

Savannah concentrated on the thought of Sam possibly bleeding slowly to death if she didn't see what she could do to help. The smell of petrol was very strong and she shied away from the thought of the car sitting in a pool of petrol under the back seat.

She pushed her arms in front of her body, stretched over her head like a springboard diver, until she could gain purchase on the seat in front of her. Theo's hands helped her hips and legs concertina in after her until she was almost jammed in the foot space behind the front seat.

She had a sudden trapped feeling and it took a few rapid breaths before she could slam the lid back on the surge of adrenaline. She squirmed until she could

turn and scrunchingly sit—half lie—along the back
seat with her head next to the child seat.

'Are you all right, Savannah?' Theo's voice was
strained and she spared a thought for the man whose
son was trapped beside her. She'd rather be here.

She could finally lift her head and see the side of
Sam's head. His eyes were still closed and she
reached across to feel the pulse at his throat. It was
there, weak and rapid, but it was there.

'He's alive, Theo.' She could hear the tears in her
voice and she swallowed a sob. 'Pulse weak and at
least a hundred and twenty.' She rested her hand on
Sam's chest and felt his rapid breaths. 'Respirations
about forty and shallow.' She swept his face and
scalp. 'Can't feel any bumps or lumps from a head
injury.' She started to run her hands over his limbs.
'I'll check for bleeding.'

Her shoulder throbbed from the previous week's
injury as she leant most of her own body weight on
it. She had to curl at an angle to be able to reach all
four of Sam's limbs. Her heart tripped when she felt
a warm dampness under the leg nearest the door. His
rapid pulse had already alerted her to the possibility
of haemorrhage.

'I need a pad and bandage. Major bleed right lower
leg.' Her own respirations increased in pace in the
restricted space and her brain was starting to clamber
for the right to be outside and unconfined.

'I can hear a car. Is it the rescue service?'

'No, sweetheart. I sent the truck driver to bring my
car down here with my doctor's bag in it in case

anything could be used. We'll use the headlights until
the others get hcre.'

'How much longer before they get here, Theo?'

Theo could hear the tendrils of panic in Savannah's
voice and he cursed his own large size which hadn't
let him do what Savannah had so selflessly done.
She'd risked her life. Later he'd think about how he
hadn't been willing to risk telling her about the child
she was trying to save.

'Another ten minutes at least. It will be dark by
then.'

Please, God, let Sam live. And don't let anything
happen to Savannah.

The driver slithered back down beside him with his
black doctor's bag.

Theo snapped it open and removed a thick pad and
crêpe bandage. 'Put out your hand, Savannah.'

He leaned into the window space and found her
hand. He squeezed it, trying to convey how much he
admired her courage. She took the bandage, and her
shoulder and arm protested at the gyrations she was
putting it through.

'You'd better blinking well stay in your socket, you
mongrel,' she muttered, as she extended herself again
to hold the pad in place while she bandaged the thin
little leg that had skipped so joyfully less than an hour
ago.

'The bandage is on and I think the bleeding is slow-
ing. His pulse is maybe a little faster but he could be
waking up a little. Sam? Sam? Can you hear me?'

She heard his little whimper with a huge sigh of
relief. Now she needed to keep him calm. 'It's OK,

sweetheart. It's Savannah. Just close your eyes again and I'll talk to you until the men come and get us out. Daddy's just outside and Mummy is, too. They'll give you a big cuddle as soon as the men come and make a door in the roof.'

'My leg hurts.' His voice was sleepy and Savannah worried at her lip, hearing the weakness in it.

'I know, Sam. Daddy will fix it soon.' The blood loss was too much for a young child to sustain. 'Theo, are you there?'

'Yes!'

'Have you equipment for cannulation? He needs fluids until you get him out.'

'Sweet Jesus, please.' She heard his whisper and closed her eyes at his pain.

If she hadn't heard it she wouldn't have been able to tell from his next response. 'I've one flask of intravenous fluid in my bag and more at home. Someone could get that while you start the first one. We don't want to overload him either. What are your chances of getting a cannula in with the access you have?'

'He's drowsy, his left arm is in front of me and I should be able to slide one in without too much difficulty. I need more light, though.'

The next half-hour was a time Savannah preferred to forget. She managed to get the intravenous line in on the second attempt, more by feel than sight. Each whimper from Sam made the tears run down her cheeks. But it was all worth it when Theo said it was working at his end of the tubing, so she must have done it right.

She bandaged a little board onto Sam's arm to stop him bending it and dislodging the drip. But he wasn't moving much.

They heard the rescue sirens a long time before the vehicles arrived because the sound bounced up the winding valley. Eventually Savannah heard vehicles themselves, more voices and the sounds of preparation to get them out. Great metal pincers were used to open the roof of the car like a sardine tin. The noise was horrible. And then the light streamed in.

'You first, Savannah.' She raised her eyes to the bright lights above her and brought up her arms. Theo reached in and plucked her from the confined space. He gave her a brief, fierce hug and then passed her back to an emergency worker. Her legs were tingling and half-asleep and the man supported her as she stood, swaying, to one side so she could see what was going on.

Savannah had undone the seat belt holding the child seat in place earlier and Theo cut the top strap to lift Sam out, still strapped in his seat like a splint. It was the safest way to move him.

The look on Theo's face as he searched his son's face made fresh tears flow down Savannah's face. His voice was hoarse.

'Sam? It's Daddy. Can you open your eyes?' There was no response. One of the paramedics reached down to take the car seat but Theo tightened his arms around it and strode straight to the ambulance and climbed in. 'I'll check him on the way. Let's move.'

That ambulance pulled away and a second stood, waiting to leave. 'I'll help you up onto the road,' the emergency worker suggested. 'The other lady is in the back of the second ambulance and wants to see you.'

Savannah had forgotten about Marie.

Theo's ex-wife was lying, wan-faced, on a stretcher, with a white bandage around her head. They were getting ready to leave.

Her voice trembled. 'They said Sam's alive. Thank God.' She reached for Savannah's hand. 'I was terrified the car was going to explode. I'm sorry. Thank you for being with Sam.'

She put the back of the other dust-laden hand over her eyes. 'I'm not a good mother.' She gave a small bitter laugh and let go of Savannah's hand. 'Theo's always wanted Sam and I've enjoyed having the power over him more than I've enjoyed being a mother. He can have him. The court was going to take him soon, anyway.'

Savannah didn't know what to say. She wasn't angry with Marie any more, just sad for Theo who'd missed out on time with his son because of this woman's power game. And sad for a woman who didn't appreciate the gift she had just given away.

'Ready?' The ambulance officer patted her shoulder and gestured that he wanted to shut the door and leave.

Savannah blinked and focussed on the uniformed man before she stepped back. 'Yes, thanks. Goodbye, Marie.' Marie turned her face away and the door shut. Savannah watched the tail-lights disappear. She turned back to the scene.

Policemen were talking to the truck driver and the rescue crews had started to clear up their equipment.

Savannah walked over to Theo's cruiser and climbed in. It smelt of Theo. She imagined how he would be feeling at that moment. She started the car and drove up to the house to shower and change. Her shoulder ached but her mind kept seeing Sam's white face in the car seat as Theo left. She had to go to them.

When she arrived at the hospital an hour later, Sam was in Intensive Care but stable. He'd needed a blood transfusion and stitches to his leg but had escaped more serious injury. Theo sat beside his bed. His head was bowed and he held his son's hand in his. When Savannah walked in he looked up.

'I knew you'd come,' he said, and tucked Sam's hand under the sheet before standing up. He held out his arms and she moved into them to be crushed against him. She buried her face in his shirt where she could hear his heart thumping and feel his fingers digging into her.

Then his hands loosened as if he'd become aware of the strength of his grip. His voice was hoarse. 'I'm sorry.'

He rubbed the area as if to rub a bruise away and she caught his fingers. 'Did I hurt you?'

'No, and it wouldn't matter.' She gazed into his face and saw the strain of the day reflected in his beautiful eyes. 'They said he'd be fine.'

'He nearly bled to death.' He let go of her and walked away, before turning and coming back to stand in front of her. 'If you hadn't bandaged his leg and started the IV fluids, he wouldn't have survived until they cut him out.'

She tried to lighten the memories he held of that horrific time. 'You would have gone in if you didn't have such lovely big shoulders.' She rested her hands on them.

His thick, dark lashes came down as if he couldn't bear her to see what he'd been feeling, and she touched his cheek and let her arms fall.

She bit her lip. 'Have you seen Marie?'

His eyes snapped open. He stiffened and stepped back. The harshness in his voice crackled with suppressed emotion. 'I really couldn't trust myself at the moment.'

'I've seen her. She's sorry and she accepts that Sam should live with you. Is that what you want?'

He stared at her as if he couldn't believe it. 'Now she says that. When it's almost too late. She doesn't mean it. It's all I've wanted for the last two years.'

'Then you've got what you want. She means it.' She touched his arm. 'You'll be a wonderful father.' She kissed his cheek and turned for the door. The rest could wait. 'Have some time with your son. I'll run you home when you're ready.'

Theo watched her as she walked away. Then he glanced at Sam, lying peacefully asleep now as the blood dripped slowly into his veins to restore him to health.

'Savannah. Wait.' He strode across and caught her arm. 'Sit for a minute.' He urged her back to the chair he'd been sitting in when she'd arrived. When she was seated he crouched down beside her and took her hand.

'I know this probably isn't the time, but the last month has been so crazy that heaven knows what else could happen before I get another chance to say this.' She half smiled at the truth of his statement.

He squeezed her hand. 'You demand nothing, yet you're capable of the ultimate sacrifice because that's the type of woman you are. Sam may have been all I wanted for the last two years but, after meeting you again, I want more. I want it all.'

He lifted her hand and kissed the inside of her wrist. 'I don't just want to be a father. I could be a wonderful husband, too. I want to marry you. If you could think of taking us on?'

Savannah closed her eyes. Marriage to Theo. Commitment to be together. Her first impulse was to say yes to the chance of spending her life with Theo and his son. But was she being fair when he was vulnerable from Sam's accident?

'Are you sure you're not mixing gratitude for need here, Theo? It's been a huge day. If you felt that strongly, why didn't you tell me about Sam before? I was so scared I'd lost you when Marie turned up with Sam and said you were going to be a family again.'

He looked across at his sleeping son and back at her. 'I'm sorry. I've been obsessed with all the time I've missed with him. To talk about him to other people would have been too much to bear. Then I met you again and now I have two obsessions.'

He stroked her cheek. 'There's magic between us,

Savannah. I feel alive when I'm with you and I've spoken of things to you that I hadn't told anyone.'

She felt her heart squeeze at his mention of magic. She tried to be rational.

'As for telling you about Sam, I intended to. But things kept happening. I did try on Thursday night. I was going to ask you to marry me after I told you about Sam. I'd been working around to it when you suddenly told me about Greg and Amelia and how you hated that you'd only been useful until they didn't need you any more.'

He looked rueful. 'So I backed off from that confession and decided to make sure you knew I loved you for yourself before I asked you to help take on my ready-made family.'

She could feel the knot of pain dissolving with his words. 'Reassure me on the middle bit again, Theo. After the confession and before the family?'

Theo smiled and the tenderness and desire and love in his face hit her like a beam of light.

'You mean the part where I said I love you for yourself?' He took both her hands in his and pulled her close. 'You're the woman of my dreams. I love you. I will always love you because of the woman you are. Be my wife.'

EPILOGUE

ONE year later Savannah waved goodbye to one of the three Scottish doctors looking up the latest information on the computer. Her other hand was entwined in her husband's as Theo walked her towards her car.

'So how do you feel after your last shift? How long, do you think, before you decide to come back?' He smiled down at her rounded tummy under the maternity smock. 'You've organised us all and the department is finally running how you wanted it.'

She grinned cheekily up at him. 'Not for a while—but I'll be back. I don't regret giving up work. The hospital's been glowingly accredited as a safe and efficient workplace. The emergency care here is top of the line and my work dream has been realised.'

She squeezed his fingers. 'I've my own organising to do before Sam's sister or brother makes an appearance.' She brushed the black strands of hair out of her eyes. The jacarandas were in flower in the hospital gardens. They reminded her of home. Her home with Theo and Sam.

She gazed up at her handsome husband, so tall and sure and content. 'My other dream just keeps getting better.' She stood on tiptoe and he bent down to meet her lips with his. 'I'll see you when you get home.'

His mouth curved. 'I love you.'

She carried his smile and his words and his baby home with her.

Modern Romance™
...seduction and
passion guaranteed

Tender Romance™
...love affairs that
last a lifetime

Sensual Romance™
...sassy, sexy and
seductive

Blaze™
...sultry days and
steamy nights

Medical Romance™
...medical drama on
the pulse

Historical Romance™
...rich, vivid and
passionate

29 new titles every month.

*With all kinds of Romance for
every kind of mood...*

MILLS & BOON®

Makes any time special™

MAT4

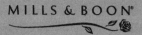

Medical Romance™

A CHRISTMAS TO REMEMBER *by Margaret Barker*

Part 3 of Highdale Practice series

Dr Nicky Devlin sees Jason Carmichael's desire for her as the perfect chance to repay him for the pain that he has caused her friend. In the run-up to Christmas she realises she loves Jason and the accusations against him turn out to be lies. How can she convince him that her feelings are real after all?

THE DOCTOR'S DILEMMA *by Lucy Clark*

Part 3 of The McElroys trilogy

Falling in love is definitely not on the agenda for ambitious bachelor Dr Joel McElroy. But living and working with the warm-hearted Kirsten Doyle reveals to Joel that she needs some TLC herself. With the arrival of Kirsten's orphaned niece, Joel finds himself drawing closer to this ready-made family—and facing a dilemma…

THE BABY ISSUE *by Jennifer Taylor*

Part 2 of A Cheshire Practice series

Practice Nurse Anna Clemence has tried to keep her pregnancy from gorgeous Dr Ben Cole, but in his desire to get closer to her, he discovers a closely guarded secret. Now he has to convince Anna that he can love this baby who is biologically neither his nor hers.

On sale 7th December 2001

Available at most branches of WH Smith, Tesco, Martins, Borders, Eason, Sainsbury's and most good paperback bookshops.

1101/03b

MILLS & BOON®

Christmas
with a Latin Lover

Three brand-new stories

Lynne Graham
Penny Jordan
Lucy Gordon

Published 19th October

Available at most branches of WH Smith,
Tesco, Martins, Borders, Eason, Sainsbury's,
and most good paperback bookshops.

OTHER NOVELS BY

PENNY JORDAN

POWER GAMES

POWER PLAY

CRUEL LEGACY

TO LOVE, HONOUR & BETRAY

THE HIDDEN YEARS

THE PERFECT SINNER

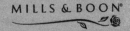

MILLS & BOON®

4 Books
and a surprise gift!

We would like to take this opportunity to thank you for reading this Mills & Boon® book by offering you the chance to take FOUR more specially selected titles from the Medical Romance™ series absolutely FREE! We're also making this offer to introduce you to the benefits of the Reader Service™—

- ★ FREE home delivery
- ★ FREE gifts and competitions
- ★ FREE monthly Newsletter
- ★ Books available before they're in the shops
- ★ Exclusive Reader Service discounts

Accepting these FREE books and gift places you under no obligation to buy; you may cancel at any time, even after receiving your free shipment. Simply complete your details below and return the entire page to the address below. *You don't even need a stamp!*

YES! Please send me 4 free Medical Romance books and a surprise gift. I understand that unless you hear from me, I will receive 6 superb new titles every month for just £2.49 each, postage and packing free. I am under no obligation to purchase any books and may cancel my subscription at any time. The free books and gift will be mine to keep in any case.

MIZEB

Ms/Mrs/Miss/Mr ....Initials.............................

BLOCK CAPITALS PLEASE

Surname...

Address...

....

....Postcode ....

Send this whole page to:
UK: The Reader Service, FREEPOST CN81, Croydon, CR9 3WZ
EIRE: The Reader Service, PO Box 4546, Kilcock, County Kildare (stamp required)

Offer not valid to current Reader Service subscribers to this series. We reserve the right to refuse an application and applicants must be aged 18 years or over. Only one application per household. Terms and prices subject to change without notice. Offer expires 31st May 2002. As a result of this application, you may receive offers from other carefully selected companies. If you would prefer not to share in this opportunity please write to The Data Manager at the address above.

Mills & Boon® is a registered trademark owned by Harlequin Mills & Boon Limited.
Medical Romance™ is being used as a trademark.